I0687339

Five Years Wasted

Copyright © 2018

All right reserved. No part of this book may be reproduced in any form or by any electronic or mechanical means, including storage and retrieval systems, without permission in writing from the publisher, except by reviewers, who may quote brief passages in a review.

ISBN: 978-1-7325887-7-6

Copyright Office Registration Number: TXu 2-093-592

Any references to historical events, real people, or real places are used fictitiously. Names, characters, and places are products of the author's imagination.

Cover image by Jenna Luciani

www.michaelpsapp.com

To my Mom
The reason why this book exists.

Table of Contents

Chapter 1

7:00 a.m. The alarm on my phone goes off. It was pretty stupid to put dubstep as my alarm. It's good to listen to in the afternoon or night but in the morning it's just one annoying noise. I roll out of bed, nearly forgetting to put my legs down to catch me. I'm super tired and I nearly ate it not one foot away from my bed, not a good start. I take a quick shower. I have to hurry, I got a long day of driving ahead of me.

I run downstairs. My parents are already up. My mom has made me breakfast. Sausage and pancakes. I am going to miss someone else making me food when I wake up. I have the feeling that I won't be making food like this in the morning.

"My little boy is growing up," she says, tears starting to run down her face. She walks over to me and grabs me tight.

"Let the boy go Maggie," my father says as he continues to read the paper with TV news as background noise.

He doesn't seem like he cares a bit that I am leaving for college. Mom is still holding me tight as I try to get free. I wish that they would trade enthusiasm for my departure so that she isn't so clingy and he isn't so detached.

I eat my meal quick and run back up to my room to brush my teeth. Grabbing what I haven't already thrown in my car, I head down. I throw my bag in my car and I am immediately attacked by my mom again. She is not handling this well. I look over to my father who seems too occupied with a bird flying overhead.

"Well, you better get going if you are going to make it on time," says my father as he looks down at his watch.

"Don't push him away," she says looking at my father angrily.

"He will be back for Christmas."

"What about Thanksgiving?" I ask.

"You should focus on school for the first semester. Coming home will just screw you up."

I say bye to the parents and jump in my car, a 2000 white Beemer, not a bad car for a college freshman. I set my iPod to my road mix and turn out of my driveway. In the rearview mirror I can see Mom waving while my father walks back inside. I don't really understand why he seems so unconcerned with me leaving for college. It's because of them that I am even going.

About four months ago I got accepted to a California university. Mom was so excited, like I had just won the lottery of something. It's just college, it's not like I just got a chance to fly to Mars. My father looked at me as if he was glad I didn't screw up. They don't know it but I only applied to one college. I really have no desire to go to college at all. I was happy where I was and I didn't want to spend money on college right now. I kept hearing horror stories and I figured I'd rather take a year off and see what my friends from high school would say their first year was like.

I had a decent job at a department store. Nothing flashy, but me and the manager were a lot alike so working there was pretty much like second nature – never going into work mad that I was there, doing my work, and then going home. Working there for the last two years I had earned the ability to pick when I worked, never having to open the store the day after I closed it. While some of the employees complained about their hours, I enjoyed mine. I didn't mind that I didn't have health insurance. I was on my parents' that they got from their company, so I didn't have to have 40 hours every week.

The one good thing about leaving was this new guy that started to work at the store. Total loser. I don't know why he got hired. Out of all the people in the world this is not a guy you expect to do a good job at anything. At first I thought my manager was mad at me for putting in my two weeks notice, like it was some kind insult leaving him. He made me show the new guy the ropes and for the last two days I worked there he followed me around the entire time. I think my IQ dropped a dozen points in those two days.

Rickie was this moron's name. He was a high school dropout who smelled like he just smoked a joint. I'm just saying, if you are going to smoke weed you should probably take a shower before work. The first day I went over safety protocol in the backroom. I moved the ladder over and was pointing out that whenever the ladder is not in use you have to put up this chain to block the way.

"Like police tape. No one cross," said Rickie giving an undeserved chuckle, his eyes glazed over.

I just ignored it and told him not to stack any boxes over six high. Too high and they fall over and could hurt someone.

"Yeah, yeah don't want to get too high. That's always never good." He gave me a nudge and a wink. I think he was trying to be funny.

I really wonder if the manager even met this guy before hiring him. I've never done drugs before but I'm pretty sure this guy is completely baked all the time. Just glad I never have to see that idiot again. There are some people in this world you wonder how they lasted this long. It wouldn't surprise me if he got hit by a bus thinking it was a giant dog asking him for a hug.

Crap! Freaking stupid!

Just great! Not even out of Utah and I'm already trapped on the freeway. Bumper to bumper on the 15. I try to see what the problem is but the line of cars is too long. If only I had a freaking smart phone I could look up a different way to go. All I got is this Google maps directions printout that just says take the 15 from Utah to California pretty much. A lot of help that is, I have to get to the dorms by 8:00 pm or I have to wait for the morning to get into my dorm room.

I really don't want to go to college. Just seems like a lot of work for nothing, but my mom went and my father went and it's a family tradition or some crap like that. They expect me to go and graduate with a degree in either Management or Finance so that I can one day take over their company.

My mom is a real estate agent and my father builds homes. They call themselves the "one-two punch of the home industry." All they ever wanted was for me to go to college so that I could go to work for them and help grow the company. For the first few years they talked about it I was excited. I thought, hey, if I work for my parents and I can have a home like them and not have to worry about a job. Now I just think, crap, now I have to see them every time I go to work.

I once helped my mom with some stuff my sophomore year in high school. That was the turning point in my desire to be a part of the "Family Business." I thought I would help her with showing the houses and sitting in on the negotiations. Man was I wrong. Instead of doing the stuff I was interested in, I ended up just doing flyer crap. For an entire summer I had to make fliers, print them out, and distribute them. She was too cheap to just send them in the mail to potential customers so I had to go driveway to driveway slipping the fliers into the mailbox. I would walk around six miles a day putting flyers in the mailboxes. Worst of all I had to make sure I delivered something like 300 flyers before 3:00 pm every day so that people got the flyer when they got their mail.

She never told me how much help the flyers were but she had no trouble telling me how I wasn't doing my best on a job I hated. The first time I went around to houses I printed out fliers and threw them in all the boxes. At dinner my mom tells me that she got a call off one of the fliers. I remember I was so excited thinking that I was about to get some thanks. No, instead of thanks I got reprimanded. Apparently I made a slight spelling error. Our last name is Freed and I accidently left out the D, so she got a call about Free Real Estate. Instead of telling me to just be careful I got yelled at for the entire dinner.

"I'm sorry! I was just helping you!" I said.

That wasn't the best thing to say to her and apparently I lost my pay for that day because of my attitude. I don't think you can dock pay for a bad attitude. It didn't matter anyway. After maybe 50 days of work I ended up with $200. Yeah, four bucks a day. Little three year olds in China made more than me. That's pretty depressing.

Well at least traffic is finally clearing up. Passing the accident, I see two cars, front ends torn apart. That much stoppage for that little accident. Lame. Driving a little farther I see another car flipped over. There are two medics placing a white sheet over a body. My head drops a little. Now I feel bad. Whatever, I didn't know the guy and I have to hurry up. As soon as I pass the last police car I hit the gas and get to up to 85 mph.

Driving through Nevada all I see is desert. I have been driving for seven hours now. I'm close to Vegas and I really need to take a piss. I been holding it for like two hours and I am about to burst. Jumping off the freeway I turn into the Golden Casino. Running as fast as I can without pissing my pants I get to the front door. Before I can even open the door some casino bouncer stops me.

"I am sorry but you can't go in. Anyone under 21 must be accompanied by an adult," the bouncer said. He didn't ask for an I.D. but I know I look young.

"I don't want to gamble, I just really need to pee. I have been driving since Kaysville," I tell him.

"Sorry kid, casino rules." He gives me a slight push back. Nothing painful but enough that I can feel a little pee run out.

"Dude, please I really have to go I promise I will just go to the restroom and then run straight out," I plead with the emotionless bouncer hoping he will give me a break.

"There's a convenience store about a mile down." He points to the left but there are too many roads to get an exact location.

I run back to my car but I know I can't make it any farther. I look around the full parking lot and I don't see a soul. I bend down and unzip my fly. Never peed in a parking lot. Check that off the list of things I've never done before. I'm a little surprised that no one has caught me yet, I feel like I have been peeing for at least three minutes. I zip up my fly and jump back in my car and drive off. Laughing I imagine that jerk bouncer walking to his car and slipping in it. Would serve him right for not letting me use the bathroom.

It's got to be 110 degrees outside. No amount of air conditioning can cool me down. The heat has frozen my IPod and I am stuck with listening to a Spanish radio station that is mostly static but it's better then listening to silence I guess.

What a crappy trip. I guess it was pretty stupid to think that this would be an easy drive. My father said that it would be tough but I figured he was exaggerating. Filling up my tank just over the California border, I watch as my bank account slowly gets smaller. It's ridiculous how much they can get for gas. Seriously government, instead of helping other countries fight wars how about getting gas down under three bucks a gallon. I'd be happy with that. I top off for the second time on this trip and head back on the 15.

Amazing how a few more dollars at the pump can annoy the crap out of us. My father gave me the BMW after my mom got her convertible. All I had to do was every once in a while put up for sale signs on properties my mom was selling. I thought it was the best gift ever until I got the first insurance bill. An old BMW still has a big cost associated with it. Couple thousand a year in insurance payments, a couple thousand in gas, and then a couple hundred in maintenance. Even though it's my car I have to follow their rules in maintaining it. I tell them you can wait seven thousand miles after an oil change before getting another one but they insist I get one at five thousand. If I didn't follow their rules they would make me pay them for the car. I couldn't believe that they would tie my hands like that.

It wouldn't be the first time they used money to get me to do what they want. Like I said, I didn't want to go to college. I'd rather take a year off and just work at the department store and then decide if college was for me. Heck, I probably would have gone to community college while I was taking my year off and take care of some undergrad requirements. They didn't like that idea. Something about going to one school and getting a degree was better. I think it's a class thing, you know, like social class, keeping up with the Joneses. It wouldn't look good to their friends if they said their kid was still at home and going to community college. Might look like they raised an idiot I guess. That's why they were so forceful about me going to college.

I told them I didn't want to go to college and that I couldn't get any scholarships and that I didn't think it was the right time to go for my degree. I sort of lied about the scholarship thing. I looked at a few scholarships but I didn't apply for any of them. I didn't really know how to apply for any and I didn't put much effort into it because I thought if I didn't get any they wouldn't force college. They made me a deal – if I went to college and graduated with my degree in either Management or Finance they would pay for half.

How could I not say yes to that deal? Half of my tuition paid for. I couldn't get a better deal than that. They were pretty much paying me over $100,000 to go to school. I jumped at that deal before they took it off the table and here I am. I took out some student loans and made my first payment toward my degree. Four years from now I will be a college graduate and my parents will pay me back for half. I imagine I will get a job and be able to pay off the student loan slowly. With my parents paying me $100,000 I can put a down payment on a house and move out right out of college. How many people can say that?

I finally get to the college at 7:55 pm. It's a big campus and I get lost around its edges. It's weird, I never visited beforehand but I expected more school and less commercial restaurants. Driving around for about twenty minutes I finally find the dorms. I park and grab my computer bag and walk into the front office.

There is a girl maybe a year or so older than me at the desk. She's got big headphones on and looking at the computer screen very intently. I walk up in front of her and she doesn't pay me any attention. Looking over to the computer screen I see she is watching some reality show.

"Hello!" I wave my hand to get her attention.

"What's up?" she says in a non-welcoming way. I wait until she takes off her headphones and pauses her show.

"I am here to check in. My name is Tyler Freed." I give her a smile as I fix my bag from falling off my shoulder.

"Can't help you."

"What do you mean?" I ask.

"We only can give keys out between 8:00 am and 8:00 pm. It's 8:18. You will have to come back tomorrow." She put on her headphones and goes back to watching her show.

"I just drove from Utah."

She takes off her headphones and pauses the show again. "What?" she says, frustrated with my mere presence.

"I just drove from Utah, I don't have any other place to sleep. Can't you just give me my room number so that my roommate can let me in?"

"Sorry. Only one of the Resident Directors can give out keys or tell people their room numbers and she left for the day. You will have to come back tomorrow at 8." I stop her before she puts on her headphones again.

"Can you call the RD and see if they will give you permission to give me a key?" I ask.

"She doesn't like to be disturbed during non-work hours."

"But..."

"Listen kid. You're late. You can't check in so you aren't a resident here yet. If you continue to stay here I will call campus police and they will show you out. Now leave or they will make you leave."

She puts on her headphones and goes back to watching her show. She's done with talking to me and is focused on being no help. I stand there for a moment until she looks back over and reaches for the phone. Walking out I make sure to hit the door hard with my hands to disrupt her listening to that stupid show.

I throw my bag in my car and just stand outside for a bit. Looking around I don't see anyone. I'm on the verge of collapsing. The drive was way too long and that jerk at the front desk didn't help me at all. I go to the passenger side of the car and get into the front seat. I throw my computer bag to the other side of the car and push the seat back as far as I can, which is about an inch. I can't stretch out my legs and can just tell I am going to get no sleep tonight. I keep shifting in the seat hoping to get comfortable, but nothing.

Over and over I keep telling myself, it will only get better. It will only get better.

Chapter 2

Ah! My freaking neck is killing me. I could not get comfortable at all last night. I turn on my car and roll down the windows. The car stinks. Well, I stink and since I have been in this car for nearly 24 hours, it smells. I always wondered what it would be like to sleep in a car and now I know. It's the worst thing in the world. It's 7:20 am. I got 40 minutes before the Resident Director will be in to give me my key, then I get a five minute rest before I have to go to my first class.

Grabbing my backpack I pull out my school schedule. First class English 8:30 am. Don't understand why they start the school year on a Wednesday. Can't they just start it on a Monday and make it simple?

Getting out of my car I try to get my back to crack, maybe if I lean backwards on the car trunk I can align my spine. Well, I got a crack but nope, still hurts. Watching as the other students head to their first class of the year I smile at what I see. There are a lot of hot girls here. I am slightly surprised – usually the Internet over-exaggerates. I should clear that up – when I applied for schools in southern California, I wanted to make sure I didn't go to a school with more guys than girls, and as many hot girls as possible. After a quick Internet search I found a website that ranked the schools with the best hotties. That was enough of a reason for me to apply.

I don't really care too much what my first girlfriend in college looks like, I just want to make sure I don't spend the first year single. I spent high school chasing after a girl who just led me on all four years. She made it seem like we were just a small step away from dating and then BAM! She is dating some guy on the football team and then the baseball team. Let's just say it sucked. The goal is to find a girl, really any girl, who is not friends with someone I would want to pursue the next year. Best case scenario is I date a girl and then we break up and she can't stand being at the same school as me so she transfers. That way I am free to date anyone I want without her telling them I'm not a good boyfriend. Girls just love to talk about guys to other girls, and they can blacklist you like that.

I nearly fall asleep next to my car, that's how tired I am. I look at my phone, 7:50 am. I guess I can make my way over to the dorm and just wait at the door. I grab my backpack and a small bag with clothes and walk through the parking lot. Looking around I see all the cars. I don't know if it's just me but when I go somewhere where there will be a lot of guys there, I like to look at their cars and see if I have a better one. There are a lot of beat up ones and a lot newer ones – seems like I am in the middle. That won't help with the girls.

Getting to the door I peer in and see a few people behind the desk. I go to open the door when I see the hours of operation on the door. 7:00 a.m. – 8:00 p.m. Seven! They open at seven! That idiot last night said eight. I could have had my key an hour ago. That's just great! I wasted almost an hour in my car making my back worse when I could have slept in my bed for an hour before class. "Forget it," I tell myself as I walk in. I don't want to yell at this guy at the desk today for the idiot girl last night.

"Morning," says the guy at the front desk. I walk closer to him. "You look terrible dude."

"Yeah, well I had to sleep in my car," I tell him. I drop my bag on the counter and pull out my paperwork and hand it to him.

"Why did you sleep in your car?" he asks as he takes my paper work.

"I showed up late last night so the RD couldn't give me my key."

"Why didn't you call the RA on duty?" he asks.

"I was told that only the RD could give keys to students." He hands me back my paperwork and I put it back in to my bag.

He gets up and walks over to a big plastic tub. "The RA on duty could have checked you in last night and given you the key."

I stick my tongue between my teeth and bite hard. Part of me wants to go find that girl who sent me away last night and throw her through a window, the other part of me wants to collapse right here on the desk. "The girl at the desk last night didn't say anything about the RA."

He looks through a bunch of files in the tub. "Well, sorry for the misunderstanding. A lot of the RAs this year are new so they don't really know all the rules." He pulls out a yellow envelope with my last name on it and walks back over to the front counter. "You're in C building. Just go out that door and follow the path left. Then go up the stairs to the third floor and look for your room number. If your roommate is in you should ask him for help with your stuff."

I look at him puzzled as I move my tongue away from my mashing teeth. "Why do I need help with my stuff?"

"Elevators on the fritz so it's been disabled."

"Great," I say sarcastically.

"You will get use to it, the elevators on campus suck too. A little advice. Use the stairs. I hear a lot of stories of students missing class because they are stuck inside.

I give him a nod, pick up my bag, and head out the door. There are a lot of couches in here and I just want to pass out on one. I can't though. I got my first class in 30 minutes. I don't open the door six inches and I hear a girl scream.

"Woo, careful," the girl says.

"Sorry," I say before she can finish.

Holding the door for her, she looks at me as if she's thinking I might try to slam the door on her.

She walks through quickly and I exit right after.

Getting to the stairs of building C, the first thing I see is a stack of ten beer cans in a pyramid shape blocking the way up. I'm tempted to kick them. It would get a lot of anger out but I choose not to. I'm not against drinking, hell I have never had a drink, and I'm hoping that my first drink will be at some party with a lot of drinks. I hear the stories of college girls who drink too much and make out with guys they normally wouldn't if they were sober. I might not be the best looking guy in the world but I'm not ugly. I'm like a seven on a scale of 1 – 10. Just got to figure out how many drinks it takes a 10 to have before I make a move on this future 10 I meet to make sure the odds are in my favor.

I reach my floor and nearly fall over. I am really feeling the affects of sleeping in my car.

A guy pops out of one of the rooms on the right. He looks at me and walks against the wall to stay away from me. "Dude, hungover the first day of classes, bad idea." He walks down the stairs.

Hungover? I look hungover? Great. Looking at my door I open up the yellow envelope to grab the key. A keycard. I don't like keycards, I'd rather they gave me a metal key. Before I can open the door it opens.

There in the doorway is a slightly awake guy standing looking at me. He has dreads to his shoulders with some beads woven in his hair.

"What are you doing?" he says.

I can tell he doesn't know I am his roommate. "Tyler Freed," I say reaching out my hand to shake his hand. "I'm your roommate."

"Really?" he says with disappointment in his voice as he looks down at my extended hand. I'm stunned that he is already upset with me as his roommate. He doesn't even know me and he hates me. This won't be a good year. "I thought you weren't going to show up and I have the place to myself."

"Oh," I pull back my hand. "Well, I'm here now."

"All right." He pushes past me to get out of the room. I watch as he walks down the hallway and down the stairs.

I don't know what confuses me more. The fact that he didn't introduce himself, or that white guys think that they can pull off dreads. Hell! Only the dude from Korn was able to pull off dreads and that's cause he was a freaking stud of an artist. Grabbing the door before it closes, I take my first steps into my dorm room.

It smells. That's saying something since I haven't taken a shower in over a day and whatever is stinking up this place is overwhelming my smell. I open up window as fast as I can. Three inches, that's as far as I can open up the window. My first thought is some idiot must have jumped out of the window and the school got sued so now all the windows are rigged to only open so far.

Turning I look at the tiny 10 by 10 room. There are two beds on either side of the walls, two desks at the foot of the beds, and two closets that barely can hold two weeks worth of clothes. I am thankful I brought duffle bags instead of suitcases, I would have nowhere to put them and would have to store them in my car all semester. Already I am having trouble figuring out which bed is mine and which one belongs to Dreadlocks. I don't know his name yet so until he tells me it will be Dreadlocks. On the left bed there is a pillow and some clothes but on the other there is a blanket and a suitcase. Kind of an even split but I pick the one on the right. If I'm wrong I guess I will just move my stuff. A little thing like a mistaken bed isn't worth fighting over.

Looking at my phone, it's 8:10 a.m. I got 20 minutes until my first class. Grabbing my backpack I look down and quickly drop it. I can't go to class smelling and looking like I'm hung over. Getting a towel and some fresh clothes I leave the dorm room and head to the showers. Walking down the hallway I discover that my room is the farthest away from the showers. Every day I'm going to have to walk nearly a block to take a shower. Maybe it just feels long because I'm so tired.

Jumping in the shower I turn the water on. I'm quickly greeted with what feels like a barrage of icicles. Nearly falling out of the shower I stand next to the shower curtain, reaching for the handle to turn the water to hot. I turn but it is already at the highest setting. I wait for something like five minutes before it finally gets hot. The water falls on my head as I just stand there. If only I could just sleep like this. As the water wakes me I start to realize the gooey texture of the floor. It's kind of like a thin layer of cream cheese. I can feel it sticking to my feet. My body may be getting clean but my feet are definitely not. There is another thing I realize – the water is crap. It's not filtered and it has the taste of metal. Unless I'm in the shower with a girl I don't think I'm going to have a good time in here.

Turning off the water I dry off and hop out. I walk over to the sink and grab a paper towel and wipe my feet. They feel a little cleaner but not much. I get dressed right as another guy walks in. He gets in the shower wearing sandals. "That's what you do," I say quietly to myself.

"You talking to me?" the guy says.

Quickly I respond. "No, just talking to myself dude." I head back to my room and throw my towel over the chair and grab my back.

"Frick!" I scream, looking at my phone. 8:25 a.m. I got five minutes to get to my first class. Grabbing my bag I run out the room and down the stairs nearly clipping someone on the second floor. Running so fast I don't even have time to apologize. I run through the dorm administration building, the realization I am late wakes me from my zombie-like state.

"Hey no running in the admin building!" a voice screams at me.

No time to respond as I am already out the door and running through the parking lot. I run across the campus until I reach Clarence Hall, where my English class is. Giving my phone a quick look. 8:40 am. Ten minutes late. That's not so bad I think before I walk in.

Opening the door I see all eyes on me. The students look at me as if they were stunned to see me. Looking over to the teacher she looks like she is just about to kill me. Standing still I hope that she will turn away from me so I can take a seat.

"Five points deducted," she says.

"What?" I say.

"You were late."

"It's the first day. Can I get a break?" I say with a smile on my face hoping she is joking. No one can be this strict on the first day I think.

"No exceptions. You are not in high school anymore." Turning to the other students. "You are adults now, so act like it." She turns to write on the whiteboard. She writes: Tardiness – Five point deduction.

Great, apparently I showed up at the perfect time to prove her point about showing up late. I walk over and take my seat next to a familiar face. It's the girl I nearly smacked with the door down at the dorms.

"Hard day," she whispers to me.

"You have no idea," I respond.

"Quiet while I am talking!" the teacher turns and says to me in a forceful tone.

I look at the girl next to me and she gives me a pity smile. Looking at the whiteboard I see a list of rules. Silence phones. No texting. No late assignments. No tardiness. No food or drinks.

After she finishes writing she hands out a syllabus to the class. Going to the end of each row she hands a stack of papers for us to pass down. When she reaches my row she glares at me. She walks back to the front and leans against her desk

"My name is Dr. Mary Dixon. I got my degree in literature at BYU and I enjoy hiking on the weekends. I like to start my class by setting the rules, handing out the syllabus, and then learning a little about my class. So let's go around." Pointing to the person in the top back corner. "You start. Tell me your name, major, and something you like to do on the weekends."

"Tom, undecided, and I like to surf," says the student apparently named Tom.

"That's neat," says Dr. Dixon. "You?" she says pointing to the student next to Tom.

This goes on for a while as I listen to the names of something like 50 students. We reach the girl next to me.

"Emily, Business, and I like to play FPS games," she says.

"FPS?" Dr. Dixon asks.

"First Person Shooter," she responds.

"Oh, okay." Dr. Dixon's calm face gets a little dark as she turns to look at me.

"Tyler, Business, and I play a lot of video games."

Dr. Dixon just looks at me and, with a little hate in her voice, looks at the middle of the room and says, "All right, that's all for today. Look at the syllabus and I will see you next week."

I look at the clock. 8:58 am. The class was a total of 28 minutes the first day and all I got from it was a syllabus and the name of everyone in the class. Oh, and the scorn of the teacher and I'm starting the year with an F.

"What you got next?" Emily asks me.

She catches me off guard as I get up from my seat. I pull out my schedule and look at it. Math 150 at 10 o'clock.

"Hey me too, I'll save you a seat. Try not to be late this time," she says as she walks out of the room.

"I'll try," I say flirtatiously back at her.

I check her out from behind. Not bad. Picking up my bag I leave the classroom. There's a lot of time to kill before my next class so I decide to go unpack my car. It takes twenty minutes to walk from my English class to the parking lot in front of the dorms, I need to remember that. Five bags. I have difficulty with two at a time so I know I will be making three trips, cussing at the elevator for being broken with the last flight of stairs. Hopefully the roommate is there and he can help me with the last trip.

Opening the door I see my roommate on top of a girl on the bed I put my stuff on.

"Oh," I call out to give the two a little warning of my presence.

"Dude, what the heck!" he calls back. "Get out of my room!"

He is now standing next to his bed, the girl has propped herself up and is looking at me but more through me. I don't think she even cares that I am in there. She is not an attractive girl, which makes me think that my roommate went for the first girl that smiled at him. Her hair is all chopped up and not even, so I think it's safe to say that she cuts it herself. I can already tell that I hate this girl by the way she dresses. She's wearing jean shorts that are tattered at the bottom like she cut them herself, and is wearing a shirt that is three sizes too small.

"I remember you," he says as he walks closer to me. "You are the freak who was standing outside my door."

"Yeah, I'm your roommate," I say. He looks at me for a second in disbelief. What a freak I have as a roommate.

"Are you the one who moved my stuff?"

I'm guessing he is talking about moving the stuff off the bed. Which means I was wrong guessing which one was his. "Yeah, I thought that one was yours."

"Dude don't touch my stuff."

"Sorry dude," I say calmly to him but more just trying to be discreet in my mocking. "I took a guess 'cause there was stuff on both."

"Make sure it doesn't happen again." I have the urge to pop him in the lip but I think he is just trying to be tough in front of the girl.

"No worries."

"Okay, good. If you'll excuse us, we are going to need some space." He goes back and lays and is about to kiss his girl like I'm not even there. "Hey I got three more bags in my car I need to bring up."

He looks at me as if I just killed his puppy. "Do you need them up here this second?"

"Well not this second..." I start.

"Then it can wait, now give me some space dude." He goes back to making out with his girl...thing.

I drop my bags on my new bed and leave the room, making sure to slam the door louder then needed. "Should have hit him," I say quietly. It's probably not the best thing to knock out your roommate the first day of school, even if he deserves it.

There are a few people walking in and out of rooms. Tempted just to knock on the first room and just say to them: "Hey, my name's Tyler. My roommate is making out with some skank in my room. Mind if I chill in here till I got to go to class?" Ha! That would be awesome if I could pull that off. I'm not that smooth, plus the door I knock on would probably belong to the roommate of the skank.

Forget it. Going down to the administration building of the dorms I find a couch and decide just to chill there, maybe start a conversation with one of the guys or girls that walk by.

Frick! I fell asleep. Still completely drained from yesterday's drive and last night's lack of sleep. Desperately searching for my phone I nearly fall off the couch. Somehow my phone got under the couch. Looking at it I see the time. 9:59 am. Late again. Part of me wonders if I should just skip today, but I can't because that girl is saving me a seat. For the second time today I am running as fast as I can to class. Getting to class I open the door expecting another scorn and lost of points from this teacher. All that looks at me are about three dozen students. I turn to the front of the room and see no teacher. Looking at my phone I see that it's 10:06. Turning back I see the girl giving me a wave.

"Thanks for saving me a seat," I say.

"Are you just going to be late every time?" she asks.

"It looks like it," I answer. "By the way I'm Tyler."

"Emily, but you should remember that from the last class," she responds smiling. "So why are you always running late?"

"Long story."

"Well what happened?"

"It's not that interesting."

"Please, the teacher isn't here," she comes in close and whispers. "And everyone else is being quiet." Returning to normal volume. "So hurry up."

I tell her the story from me leaving Utah and coming here, leaving out the part about pissing in the parking lot of a casino and the rude RA. Turns out she also lives in the dorm in building A. Then I tell her about my roommate and pretty much being kicked out and finally telling her I fell asleep in the administration building of the dorms and had to run here.

"It's called the Commons Building," she says.

"What is?"

"The dorm's administration building. It's called the Commons Building or just Commons."

Right as she finishes a middle-aged Indian man walks into the classroom. Not the tribal Indians but the outsource one. He's got a tan satchel on one shoulder and a Starbucks coffee. At first I don't think he's the teacher until he drops his bag on the front desk by the whiteboard. After all who would think a college teacher would wear jeans and a yellow polo to class.

He turns to the class and just looks disappointed in what he sees. Taking a drink from his coffee he starts talking. "I'm Dr. Kurala and this is Math 150." I think that's what he said. His accent is so thick I can barely understand him.

He says some more things about something but I am not exactly sure what he said. I think it is about the grading aspects of the class but not exactly sure. I make a mental note to ask Emily what he said. She seems like she understands this guy a lot easier then me. I get a syllabus and look at it.

30% Homework

30% First Test

40% Final

Very simple grading criteria but I nearly forget to breathe as I see the 40 percent final. Forty percent are you serious! You could ace everything but if you bomb that final you are SCREWED!

"No extra credit," he says. I understood that one. Forty percent final and you don't give extra credit? Why not just fail half the class now and get it over with. "That's all for today. The drop deadline is next Friday." With that he picks up his bag and leaves.

The guy was 15 minutes late for class and then spent five minutes actually being here. Starting to think that the first day of class is a joke. I have one more class today but I am tempted just to skip it if it's like these two.

"Wait, why did he mention the drop deadline?" I ask Emily. "Do you think a lot of people fail his class?"

"He probably has to tell people," she says. "I wouldn't worry about it. You done for the day?"

"No I got Philosophy 102 at six."

"Cool, I'm done for the day but if you are hungry I'm going to go to the cafeteria."

"Sure." I haven't eaten all day. The last food I had was somewhere after the California border, and that was just a gas station burrito.

We go to the cafeteria and I learn that Emily is from Orange County. She originally wanted to go New York but lost her soccer scholarship after she broke her leg during her last season. It's amazing that she doesn't seem bitter or angry with any of it. If it were me I would have been cursing everything and everyone.

There is something about Emily. I don't know what it is but she seems like the kind of person that I have known my whole life. Just the way we talk it seems so fluid. There are no pauses or forced conversation. I know I was thinking she might be the girl I date first and get a little practice under my wings and then move on, but now I'm thinking I'd rather keep this one as a friend.

We grab food and talk for a few hours and then she heads back to the dorms and I decide I want to check out the library. I didn't think about asking Emily if she wanted to join me, after all I don't want to make it seem like I am dying for attention. I head to the library and find another couch to take a nap on. This time I'm smart and set an alarm fifteen minutes before class.

My phone goes off. I find it quickly and turn it off. Last class of the day, hopefully it will be like the other two and last only twenty minutes tops. The campus is dead. There are only a handful of people there and I am fairly certain that they are going home for the day.

Getting to Philosophy I am one of about 15 there. The teacher is already there sitting at the front desk reading some book with a skull on it. I don't see any words on it but I'm guessing it is some pompous piece of philosophical crap. He is an older man, if I were to put an age on it, I'd say about 60 or 65. His white hair is thinning and he is wearing a blazer and a t-shirt under it. I second-guess what I see, but low and behold, there is a cat on his shirt!

I take my seat and wait. There's five minutes left until class officially starts and he still hasn't lifted his head from his book. Looking at the clock tick closer to six I start thinking about what I want to have for dinner. *Okay, six o'clock class, out in like twenty. I can get to my car by 6:35 and get to the pizza place by 6:40 and back by 6:50. Eat it down at the Commons and if someone walks by and eyes my pizza I can offer them some and make some friends.*

6:00. As soon as the second hand hits the 12 the teacher closes his book and stands up.

"I am Dr. Mills and this is Philosophy 102." Is every teacher a doctor here? I wonder. "In this class you will learn the basics of philosophy and learn to open your mind to the inner workings of human reasoning, the inner workings of the human thought process, and have a better understanding of true knowledge. By the time you leave this class you will not just know why people make certain choices but what underlying issues inform these choices."

My first thoughts are: What the heck! This is a first year Philosophy class and he's going to teach us all this crap and then expect us to be tested on it. He hands out the syllabus and I prepare to leave, expecting he was done for the day. I'm dead wrong. As soon as I stuffed that syllabus in my bag, he turns to the white board and starts teaching. His old gravelly voice is very quiet and I feel lucky that I took a seat in the front row. If I can barely hear him I wonder if the people in the back row can even make out a word. It doesn't help that he is speaking to the board as he writes instead of looking at us.

Throughout the lecture he goes off on tangents about things that have nothing to do with philosophy. At first he was talking about red herrings and then I kind of zone out but then he says something about magic and starts talking about when he was in Vegas and saw a magic show. He talks about that show for about ten minutes. It was only after he says, "I wish I could saw a woman in half," that I realize that this isn't an analogy of anything and just a random story. Now my notes have his vacation in it. For the next two hours he talks, going off on random tangents every so often.

Glancing over to the clock on the wall, I see there's only five more minutes until class is over. I look around and nearly everyone is resting their head on their desk or nearly there. This class sucks the living life out of you but what choice do I have, I have to take Philosophy. Just have to muscle through.

All the sudden everyone packs up their stuff and gets up. I am startled for a minute, not hearing anything indicating dismissal. Grabbing my bag I leave the room, feeling more tired than I did in the morning. Curious if it's because of the previous night or that this class is just exhausting.

Going through the Commons back to my room, I am stopped by a familiar voice.

"Hey Tyler." I turn to see Emily. Instead of saying anything I just give her a wave. "Where you headed?"

"Just back to my room I guess."

"Me and a few people are going to a party. You want to come with?"

I look at the people she is going with. There are two guys and a girl. For a moment I wonder if I am intruding on a double date thing. After all being a third wheel is bad but being a fifth wheel is just torture. Studying the group I can see there is no romantic situation here. The girl is just average and the two guys have no chance at Emily.

"Sure. Sounds like fun. Just let me toss my bag in my room." I say making a motion towards the back door.

"Don't worry about it dude. Just throw it in my trunk," says one of the guys. He is tall with brown hair wearing a retro Grateful Dead shirt.

"Okay," I say as I start to follow them. We go out into the parking lot and jump into the tall guy's beat up old van. Definitely this guy has no shot with Emily, but he might have a chance with the other girl. A smile appears on my face knowing that there won't be any animosity between us over girls.

"By the way," Emily says as she tucks her hair behind her ear. "This is Matt," pointing at the driver. "Sid," pointing to the guy sitting in the front seat. "Scout," pointing to the girl next to her. Emily is in the middle of the back seat and I am on her left.

"Scout?" I ask.

"Yeah, yeah, yeah, I know it's a funny name," says Scout.

"It's just unusual," I say, hoping not to insult her or Emily.

"My mom liked To Kill a Mockingbird. At least she didn't call me Atticus."

I remember we had to read To Kill a Mockingbird in high school but I barely remember it. Well I barely remember the SparkNotes anyways.

"So where is this party?" I ask, trying to get off the girl's weird name.

"You know Los Posa Apartments? In there," says Matt.

We drove for only two minutes before we reach the apartment complex. No idea why we didn't just walk over. The complex is large but everything was smashed together. The driveways aren't really big enough for two cars. While we drive up and down looking for the apartment, I wonder if a car would come from the other direction and force us to reverse all the way back. When we finally find the apartment, there is no parking so Matt just pulls over to the side and lets us out.

"I'll be back," Matt said in an Arnold Schwarzenegger impression. A very poor impression. This is the kind of guy I think would be a good friend to have. He seems pretty cool but no threat when it comes to girls.

We make our way up to the third floor where the party is. It was only 8:30 and people are already completely trashed. There is one guy passed out on the stairs as we walked up. "Joey can't hold his vodka," says some guy. The music is blaring and is probably the most random playlist I have ever heard at any party. There is rock, rap, and sometimes some Korean pop crap.

I go to grab a beer when some guy who is completely trashed pushes into me to grab a beer for himself.

He turns and looks at me up and down. I am taken aback, as I don't know what he is thinking. "What's your problem?" he says aggressively to me.

"What?" I say taking a step to the side.

"Why you hit me?" he demands an answer.

"I didn't. We were both going for a beer and we just hit. No one's fault bro."

"Bro? Bro? I ain't your bro dude." He pushes my shoulder and stands up as straight as he can, putting his red cup down on the counter and clenching his fist. "Just say you hit me dude."

"I didn't. If anything, you hit me," I say.

This just made him angrier. If I had said sorry he probably would have left, or if I tried to distract him by saying something about his shoes he might have just walked away. But I didn't. He turns for a moment and then quickly sucker-punches me right in the face. A millisecond after being hit I was on the ground.

"WOO!" he screamed. "What now bitch!"

By the time I'm able to get to my feet the jerk is gone. I don't know where he went and no one else at the party seems like they're going to tell me. Standing, but a little woozy, I can feel my eye slowly close and become very tight. Black eye. Definitely going to have a black eye tomorrow.

"What happened?" asks Emily. Apparently she hadn't seen the whole thing and just caught me getting up off the floor.

"Some a-hole just sucker-punched me in the eye."

"Are you okay?" she asks, very concerned.

"Yeah I'm fine. Just wished he wouldn't have run off so I could return the favor," I might have made it sound like I wanted to finish the fight but I could barely see. My left eye is completely shut and my right eye is a little fuzzy as well.

"Do you need anything, like ice?"

"Nah, I'm fine." I try to act tough but I am in a lot of pain. It feels like my eye has been pushed back into my brain and I really want to cry but all my strength is going to preventing a single tear.

"Let's get out of here. Your left eye doesn't look good. Come on I'll walk you home. Wait here." She leaves and tells Scout that we are leaving and she comes back. She grabs hold of my arm. "Let's go."

We head down the stairs, passing the passed out guy. Even with fuzzy vision I can see that he now has some words drawn on his forehead. Not sure what it says but I can guess it's nothing flattering. Right as we step out to the street we see Matt running up.

"Where you guys going?" Matt said.

"Some tool punched Tyler for no reason so we are just going to head back," she says.

"Dude that sucks. You want me to drive you back?" I appreciate the offer, but I'd rather get to know Emily a little better.

"No thanks Matt," she says.

"All right. See you guys later," says Matt. He accidently nudges my arm as he passes and goes into the party.

"Be honest," Emily says as we reach the gates of the apartment complex. "Did you entice the guy to hit you or was he just a tool?"

I let out a laugh. "No it was all him. Just went for a drink and he ran into me. Then he got all mad and I tried to calm him down and he just punched me and ran off." I look at her and I think she is smiling but I'm not 100% sure of what face she is actually making. My vision isn't really the clearest right now.

"Well lucky for him I didn't see it or else I would have dropped him." I let out another laugh. "What, you don't believe me?" I don't say a word but crack a smile. Then she turns and punches me right in the gut. A huge breath of air is pushed out of my lungs and I hunch over. Her punch was hard and perfectly placed. It takes a few second for me to take a breath and I try to stand up straight but I am slightly hunched over. "Four older brothers. You learn a thing or two about fights."

"Okay, next time you can fight the guy," I say as I regain my normal breathing pattern but now my eye and my gut hurt.

We walk maybe a block or two in silence before she speaks again. "So you got your eye on any girl yet?"

I pause for a second not knowing how to answer. Not sure if I should joke and say her and see what she thinks or what. "Eh, not really. What about you? Any guys chasing after you?"

"No guys yet. I don't want to date my first year. I'd rather just survive freshman year and then start dating. Well, I mean I will allow myself the opportunity to date. I'm not trying to say that guys are flocking towards me all the time but I mean I'd rather find someone next year than this year."

"Please, I bet in high school you had a ton of guys going for you," I say as if I am teasing but I bet she did have a ton of guys she dated.

"Didn't really date in high school. I mean I did date one guy for two years but he was a jerk."

"What'd he do?" She drops her head and I know I hit a sore spot. "Oh, never mind."

"We got into different schools and he demanded I move out and just go to community college near him and apply again next year."

"And you didn't like that idea?"

"The idea was okay but it was the way he said it. Like I was just suppose to follow him." She paused and looked up at the sky for a moment. "If he didn't get angry I probably would have gone but he just started yelling at me so I just said screw it and we broke up."

"Sorry." I say it, but I don't mean it.

"Don't be. He was a jerk. At least it was in high school. What about you? Did you have a serious relationship in high school?"

For a moment I thought of just telling her I dated a girl my junior year that lasted a month before she dumped me but it seemed a little too pathetic. I want to sound cool but not like a jerk. "I dated a couple girls but nothing really worked out."

"Because of you or them?"

"Half and half I'd say," I prepare for her next question with the perfect lie but she doesn't ask.

"What do you have tomorrow?"

"Biology and California History. You in any of those?"

"Nope."

Crap, I was really hoping that she was. We get to the dorms and walk through the Commons. She guides me to building C and drops me off. We say our goodbyes and she heads to her building and I walk up to my room. I nearly trip on a few steps. As soon as I get to my bed I fall down on top of it and pass out.

Chapter 3

Ten weeks go by and I spend four days of the week completely tired and three days just trying to catch up on sleep. I don't think people understand how impossible it is to get sleep in college. All the teachers give out test and papers around the same time and they schedule classes really early. By the time I fall asleep I have to wake up three hours later to go to class. I think I have lost 5% of my total grade in English and History just because I can't wake up that early some days. Stanley, the Dreadlock douchebag of a roommate, isn't helping out either.

He is always getting on my nerves. Just the other day he got mad at me again for waking him up. Stanley's lucky he doesn't start class until noon, but he blames me for waking him up every morning because my alarm goes off. He has even complained to the RA that I keep waking him up. Such a hypocrite! I wake him up 'cause I need to go to class but he wakes me up at one in the morning drunk or high with his girlfriend. I just put in earplugs and just trying to sleep through their crap. It usually only last five minutes anyways.

I tried complaining to the RA about that but what is a guy just a year ahead of me going to say. One thing I have realized here is that the RAs are either wimps or super aggressive. I have seen RAs cry because they had to write someone up for drinking and this other RA totally go power crazy. Natalie, the overly aggressive one, made sure a guy got a strike because his roommate was drinking. His roommate is 21 and legally can drink in the dorms. The underage roommate wasn't even drinking but she still gave him a strike.

That's the problem with people who have been picked on in high school or in college – as soon as they get some kind of power they abuse it. I can just imagine what they think as they write someone up. "I am a god and I can destroy you if I so please." What idiots! Know your place. You are not better than everyone else now. Everyone hates Natalie, even the RAs, but since she is just like one of the RDs she can act however she wants. She will probably graduate and become an RD, become one of those people who just get stuck in college and never wants to give up the power they think they have over college students. Pathetic.

If it weren't for Emily I probably would have been kicked out of the dorms already. The dorms have certain rules that will get you strikes. There are a bunch of rules but really they only enforce drinking because alcohol poisoning gets them in trouble. Emily has this great sixth sense. She just has this ability to know when it was time to leave a place. We'd be drinking in someone's room and she'd be like, let's go, and I would follow. Within ten minutes a RA would knock on the door and as soon as those idiots opened the door they'd get written up. This one time we walked right past Natalie within seconds of closing the door. Natalie just looked at us with an evil stare and was like, "Did you just come out of there?" pointing at the room she was going to pass. "No," said Emily. "Why? What's up?" Natalie just pushed by us and knocked on the door. We quickly walked down the hall before she decided that we were in that room.

That's the thing – Natalie could have said she saw us leave the room and write us up. I am pretty sure if Natalie told the RD something, even if it was a lie, they would believe her.

Emily and me are two different people when it comes to school. She goes to class happy and relaxed and seems to get perfect scores on everything. Me, on the other hand, I struggle everyday just to get Cs, if I am lucky. I am barely passing Philosophy and Biology. If it wasn't for Calculus and History I'd probably get on academic probation.

I had to pull a few all-nighters this semester just to finish a few papers. English, Philosophy, and History have papers and tests at the same time. History is easy but the teachers expect me to write a ten page paper in a week. Heck, all the teachers are the same. They say that we have known about these papers since the first day of school. That's true but we don't freaking know what we are writing about until the week before. Like, come on moron, we have to rewrite it like three times because you add new criteria every couple days. By the end I have added so much bullshit to this paper that when I turn it in I don't even know what I am saying. I am just trying to get to that ten page requirement.

I think the biggest annoyance is that the teachers all think that their class takes priority over everything else. Sorry, but no it doesn't. It gets equal loathing to all the others.

In Philosophy today I get back my second test of the semester. On the first one I got a D. I don't understand. I studied hard and memorized all the definitions but still didn't pass. This second one, my grade is a C. I spent four days just focusing on this test and I got a C. It wouldn't be so bad if this idiot in my class isn't getting perfects. This guy is just like Stanley. He is a total druggie who doesn't even pay attention in class but he gets Bs on every test. I just don't understand how this brain-dead monkey gets better grades than me.

Class gets out and I chase the druggie down. Not knowing his name I just tap him on the shoulder. "Hey, how do you pass the tests?" I ask him. It sounds like an insult and I know. I don't know how to ask any other way really. How do you ask an idiot how to pass a test?

He just looks at me and his eyes just slowly drift away from me and he has to try and focus again. "What do you mean?"

He is high right now. I bet he smoked today. "I saw you get good grades on the tests and I'm struggling. Just looking to know your studying technique."

Smiling he starts to chuckle in a very creepy way. I take a very slight step back. "Study? I don't really study."

"How do you pass then?"

Turning his backpack around he opens the front pocket open slightly and shows me a bag with at least six joints in it. "I smoke one before every test. You want to buy one? Fifty dollars and I bet you pass the next test."

I wave my hand. "Nah dude, just wondering how you did it."

Zipping up his bag he gives me the peace sign and leaves. I should have known. After thinking about it, it does seem like Dr. Jackson is a little high during class. He goes off on pointless tangents all the time. Only stoners would be able to stay on board his train of thought.

Dr. Jackson walked by me and I ran to catch up to him. "Mr. Jackson!" I call out but he doesn't stop. "Mr. Jackson," I say again. I get in front of him this time so he sees me talking to him.

"It's Doctor or Professor, not Mister," he says, looking insulted.

I don't want to insult him when I need help, so I apologize. "My mistake. I was wondering if I could ask you a question. On the test..." I start but he quickly waves at me and cuts me off.

"I don't answer any questions after class. If you want to speak to me you will have to do it at office hours."

"I know but I have class during your office hours," I say.

"Well, then I guess you are at an impasse. Either come to my office hours or go to your class.

"Can I send you an email?" I ask.

"Sorry but I have office hours for a reason and it is not any of my concern if you can't make them."

Part of me just wants to kick him in the face. *You have office hours because the school requires them. I am asking for help and you are just pushing me off. No concern of yours? You jackass! I need help in your class and you won't help me. You're a dick.* But of course I can't say anything like that and all I can say to him is, "Okay."

The next day I skip my class and go to his office hours. There is a girl already there but I wiggle the handle to make sure it's not locked. It's locked and she gives me a "duh" look. We wait in silence and about five minutes after his office hours begin his door opens. I am shocked to see him in there. He knows people are waiting out here for him and he was just chilling in there. The girl goes in first and after 40 minutes she opens the door and thanks him for the help.

"Come on in," he says with regret in his voice.

"Thanks," I say to be polite.

"What can I help you with?" he asks.

"I am having trouble with the tests." He cuts me off.

"What class are you in?"

I'm surprised that he doesn't know which class I'm in after I tried talking to him yesterday. "Philosophy 102."

"I teach three classes of Philosophy 102." He looks at me like I did something wrong. He seemed happy when he talked to the girl but now that he is talking to me he acts like I killed a cat in front of him.

"Thursday at…" I start before getting cut off again.

"Okay, what's your problem?"

"Ah…well I haven't done good at all on the two tests. I study for them really hard and spend a good three or four days just studying and memorizing the definitions but I struggle on the essay part." He doesn't seem focus on what I say and his gaze travels around the room as I speak. "What I am wondering is," I say slightly louder to get his attention, "how do I study more efficiently to pass your tests?"

Looking at me he leans back in his chair and seems to be thinking very in depth about my question. "Have you tried studying better?"

What the hell! I nearly screamed at the top of my lungs cussing this idiot out. Literally biting my tongue so I didn't say what I was thinking, I wait until enough rage passes so I can ask the question in another way. "Okay, well, when it comes to the essays, is there a way I can write it better so I can answer it in a way you like?"

He continues to sit back in his chair and waits a few moments before speaking. "I give you the question, just answer it."

"That's it?" I say. I try to hold back my disgust with his answer but I can tell I let a little out. He doesn't seem to notice.

"Yeah, just study better and answer the question. Any other questions?" He gives me a slight smile as if he is happy with his answer.

"No that's it. Thank you," I shake his hand and imagine throwing him through the window. "Have a great week." As soon as I close the door behind me I give him the finger and mouth all the dirty words I know at the door. Not only did I lose points from my other class for going to his office hours, but it solved NOTHING! I do not feel confident about the final and he pretty much didn't help me with anything.

Getting back to my dorm, I open my door to see Stanley's disgusting girlfriend sleeping in his bed. I shut my eyes tight and though I want to kick her out I just sit at my desk. I put on my headphone and I start working on some Biology homework.

About half an hour goes by when suddenly a pillow hits me.

"What the hell creeper! Why you watching me sleep?" she yells at me.

The pillow knocks my headphones askew. I want to throw the pillow back at her but I toss it to the end of the bed. "I'm not. Just working on some homework in MY room."

"You were looking at me, I saw you," she insists.

"No I wasn't. What are you even doing in here? Shouldn't you leave when Stanley leaves?

"Stanley says I can stay in here whenever I want," she raises her voice at me.

Stanley enters the room quickly hearing his dirty girlfriend scream. "What's going on?" he looks at me.

"Your pervert roommate was watching me sleep," she says bringing her legs to her chest and wrapping her arms around them.

"What is wrong with you sicko?" says Stanley. Walking over to me he gives me a medium-sized push.

"I wasn't watching her. I was just doing homework," I tell him. Trying to stay calm, I just stare at him, making sure not to seem intimidated by him.

"He's lying," she screams.

"She shouldn't even be in here if you're not here!" I start to raise my voice.

"So you were watching her." He looks at me as if he caught me in a lie.

"Hell no! Why would I watch that trash sleep." With that Stanley tries to throw a punch at me. I dodge the punch and stand up quickly, pushing him back. Not realizing my headphones were connected to my laptop, it falls to the ground at the same time Stanley hits the wall. I pick up my computer and put it on the desk and take off my headphones and prepare for another one of Stanley's futile attacks. His stoner eyes are more watery then usual. He is about to cry, I can tell.

"Screw you man!" he yells at me and then runs out of the room. His girlfriend just looks shocked, staring at the door.

I turn and look at her. "You should probably go now," I say forcefully.

"You're an asshole!" she says leaving the room.

For 15 minutes I am free to work on my homework. Then the door opens and I prepare for

Stanley to either try and attack again or be so stoned he doesn't remember what happen. I turn to see him behind the RA Natalie.

"What's up?" I ask a little shaky.

"Did you hit Stanley?" asks Natalie.

"No," I respond quickly.

"Well, they have a different story," she says.

"He tried to take a swing at me and I pushed him back and then he ran away like a baby."

"That's a lie! Stanley was standing up for me and he pushed him," screamed his girlfriend.

It was at that moment I realized I have never bothered to know her name. If I did I would have called her by name but instead proceed without it. "She's lying. She got all pissed at me 'cause she thought I was watching her sleep when I was doing homework. And I wasn't! Then Stanley tried to punch me when she said I did."

Natalie just looked at me and then at Stanley who was putting on the helpless victim act. "If that's true you should have come to me first Tyler instead of taking things into your own hands."

"What? I can't go get you before knowing he's going to punch me," I say completely shocked by the stupidity of her statement.

"Don't treat me with disrespect," she says. "I am going to write you both up."

"What?" Stanley and me say in unison.

"You two will also have to talk to the RD and sign a roommate agreement so this won't happen again." With that she leaves with Stanley and his girlfriend still in the doorway. I look at them making sure not to blink. Stanley flips me off and then leaves.

For the next week Stanley stays in his girlfriend's room. The RD confirms that we had strikes against us and makes us sign a roommate contract. I can not touch Stanley in any way and the girlfriend is not allowed to spend the night or be over without Stanley. If I do touch Stanley I will be kicked out immediately. Fearing that Stanley would pull some bullshit to get me kicked out I spend most my time in other rooms or make sure that someone else is in my room during the day.

I swear if it wasn't for Emily, my anger for Stanley would just continue to boil and I would get kicked out or maybe even arrested for murder. Emily is just amazing. She is such a great person, I don't understand why she doesn't have every guy begging for a date.

The Saturday before finals I go to a study session for Calculus. I have a B going into the final so I don't really want to go but Emily says that I have to go. I go to library and see the small group around Emily. I walk over.

Emily sees me and jumps up all excited. "Tyler this James and Bee," she paused. "And this is Alice," says Emily, giving me a wink so Alice can't see.

Right away I know what she is getting at. She thinks she has found me a girl. "Hi everyone," I say coolly, trying not sound to excited. Emily slides over so I can sit next to Alice.

We spend the next two hours talking and studying for the test. Although Emily is much smarter than me in everything, she makes sure to make me look like a genius. She talks me up to the group but mostly to Alice. I feel like me and Alice have some good chemistry but, wanting to play it cool, I say I'd friend them online. The group splits off, leaving just Emily and me alone in the library.

The second that Alice is gone Emily hits me in the chest. She sure can hit hard. "Oh my gosh! She is like perfect for you, right? She is smart, well semi-smart, beautiful, and I know you didn't talk about much but you have so much in common!" She is so excited that her voice becomes higher in pitch.

"Yeah, she was cool."

"That's bull. You know you like her. Tell me she isn't perfect." I pause and smile and look down at the ground. "Win!" she yells. "Remember. Your firstborn. It's Emily. E...M...I...L...Y. You two will have such cute kids." Jumping to her feet she grabs her bag and starts walking towards the exit. Turning slightly back toward me, "Hey, I just introduced you to the mother of your children. The least you can do is buy me dinner." She waves me to follow her and I do.

Chapter 4

First semester of college ends. Finals week is both the busiest and laziest week of school. Not only do you study like crazy but you also sleep and drink more than any other time. Two finals on Monday means that I can drink Tuesday and Wednesday. However when Thursday comes around I see and talk to no one as I study. Not ten minutes after my last final I had already have a beer in me.

The best thing about the English class is the fact that our final was a paper. A six page double spaced paper on a stupid book called Life of Pi. It's one of those books that even the SparkNotes makes you crazy reading. I talk to a few people in class and they didn't read the book at all either. It seems like the only people in college who read are the ones who actually enjoy reading. Those who are required to read choose to read the SparkNotes. I wonder if colleges realize this or they just don't care as long as they continue getting the tuition checks.

I go home Saturday. I don't know why but I remember the trip being easier than it actually was. When I get home late that Saturday night, my mom wraps her arms around me like I had been gone for years at war, even though I saw her over Thanksgiving break, against my father's forceful suggestion. My father just looks at her as if nothing happened and I never left. My mom asks me the same questions over and over. I don't think she would be happy unless she was at school with me. My father just cares about one thing – did I pass?

That is the problem. I don't know if I passed. Grades won't come out until two weeks after school had ended. I have a general idea what my grades will be. History and English will be high Bs. Biology in the C range. Math C and Philosophy I am just hoping to pass. For the final, I took the class stoner's advice. I didn't get high; I thought about it, but I didn't want to take the risk on the final. I did, however, act as if I was a stoner during the essay portion. I went on a few tangents when answering the question and even used an analogy to explain an analogy. It was just the dumbest thing ever but I wasn't going to pass if I went with my non-stoner way of taking tests.

Two weeks pass and I spend a lot of my time on the computer talking to Emily and Alice. Most the time I am talking to both at the same time. Emily is very confident that Alice and me are destined to be together. I just want to date her but hey, if being destined to be together helps my chances of getting with her I am okay with it.

The three of us are all online waiting for grades to go up. Alice is nervous that she is going to flunk out. Emily doesn't seem to care. After all, she went into finals with straight As. Even if she only fills in half the answers, she still walks out with Bs.

"So freaked out right now. Seriously if I don't pass math I am going to literally die!" messages Alice.

"Don't worry you prob did fine," I message back.

She took a long time to write back. I imagine she was refreshing the page like crazy. Grades are up at 5:00 p.m. but she thinks they might come up early. While she nervously waits for grades, Emily and I have a nice conversation about what my strategy with Alice should be. That's the funny thing about flirting with a girl – there is a lot of planning. If it's not just a random hookup at a party – you have to think about your moves.

"Remember if you come on too strong you are going to scare her off, and if you do that you lose any chance," messages Emily.

"So what do you suggest?"

"Well it depends what you feel comfortable with. The easiest way is just to go to a party together and let the alcohol do its trick. The problem is that you got a bunch of other guys going to block you and then you spend the whole night trying to get her attention. You need to have her attention right away."

"I don't want to have to fight lol." I am joking but also imagining that situation. Things would work out just the way she described. I know. I have been the guy blocking other guys to talk to a girl.

"You could also just try and ask her out now."

"Like right now?" I am a little confused by the direct approach.

"Well yeah, but not online. You've got to call her."

"Nah, I don't want to do that. 'Hey want to go out? Yeah well not now...I'm in Utah now, but you know in like three weeks you want to go out?' Like that?" I hope she understands the sarcasm. The one thing I have learned is writing with a sarcastic tone is near impossible. A lot of people are so dense that they think you're stupid, or they are dumb enough to think that's what you actually mean and think you are a jerk.

"Yeah, you're right." After about a minute or so she finally starts typing again. "Okay here's the plan. Have you picked your classes yet?"

"Yeah."

"Are you good in science?"

"Yeah, I'm pretty good. Like I should get a pretty good grade in Biology." I lie, but I don't want to tell her that I am just average.

"Me and Alice are in Physics next semester with Prof. Gingreg. You need to take that class with us. When she struggles, which I bet she will, you come over to 'help her.' A couple of late night studying and BOOM! You got yourself a girlfriend."

That could work. Late night study never lasts long, and that part of your brain that says "nah that's not a good idea" doesn't speak up. Luckily I need Physics to satisfy my science requirement and I can get into the class.

"Gah!!!," Alice writes. "I PASSED MATH!"

"That's great! What you get?"

"I got a B-."

"Awesome!"

"Thanks for your help I will see you next semester." She signs off before I could say bye and don't speak to her for the rest of the break.

When I see my grades I was met with an unfortunate truth. Finals freaking suck! In history I got a B, English a C+, and Math, Biology, and Philosophy I got a C. I am lucky I somehow passed Philosophy but my grades took a straight nosedive. Any lower and I'd be repeating all the classes next semester.

"Hey what did you get?" Emily asks.

"Meh, Bs," I lie. "You?"

"Four As and a B."

Of course she almost aced everything. That seems to be her luck. I don't really talk to anyone from school until I go back. When I do get back I am met with some passive aggressive revenge from Stanley. Opening the door I'm met with a brutal attack of stink. It smells like someone set a dead skunk on fire. It is nasty. I open up the window and even spray a bunch of body spray all over the place. Looking under his bed I find what looked to be a combination of milk, chicken, and beer in a giant bowl. Definitely done on purpose. I wait all day for Stanley to return so I can confront him but he doesn't show up the first week of school. For a bit I thought he dropped out and I would have the dorm to myself. Besides the smell, it is one of the best weeks of school. Doesn't work out that way. Stanley comes back the second week just as douchey as ever.

When I finally see him I confront him. This time I am smart enough to have one of the RAs there with me. That way him and his stupid girlfriend can't collude with each other again. He is in our room just doing something on the computer. I doubt it was homework, so I text the RA to come over.

The RA walks in and looks at the confused stupid face of Stanley.

"Stanley, you left some kind of disgusting food, drink mixture under your bed over break. You need to keep your side clean. When I got back here it was disgusting and I had to buy spray to cover up the smell. I would appreciate it if you would be more respectful of our shared space and throw all food away as soon as you are done eating it," I tell him in the calmest way I could. It was hard. The entire time I wanted to just punch him in the face but I can't get kicked out of the dorms. Turning to the RA I wait for him to respond.

He closes his computer and just looks at me for a while before speaking. "I don't smell anything."

"That's because I kept the window open for a week and sprayed this place like a thousand times."

"A thousand times? That's an exaggeration and if you are exaggerating about that you are probably exaggerating about the smell." He glares at me and give me this little smile.

"Dude, I just want you to take better care of your side and clean up," I say raising my voice a little.

"Whoa dude, calm down. See he has an issue with my side of the room but I have an issue with his anger issues."

"Dude just clean your freaking side of the room." The RA has yet to say anything. He just stands there listening.

"Did anyone smell the room?"

"What?"

"Did you smell the room?" he asks the RA.

"Nope," he responds.

"Then its just hearsay. There is no proof of anything you say. You could just be trying to cause problems 'cause you don't like my girlfriend."

"This has nothing to do with your girlfriend!"

"Are you sure? You been jealous of our relationship since you first met her."

"Listen retard, just clean your damn side!"

"Whoa calm down," the RA says getting in front of me blocking my path to Stanley. He looks at me and puts his hands on my shoulders as if he is ready to stop me from fighting. "That's no way to speak to your roommate."

"But he's..." I start before being interrupted.

"Let's talk outside." The RA gives me a push to the door and we make out way out. "He's right. You have no proof that he purposely left out his food, and if he did it was probably an accident."

"Are you serious? Weren't you watching? He was playing you!"

"Tyler, I had to deal with this kind of thing last year. I know when one roommate has it out for the other. You need to settle down and just relax."

"What? Me? You think I have it out for Stanley? Have you seen his girlfriend? She's a dirty whore!" I know my anger is getting control of me but the idea that this guy who is a year older then me thinks he knows people perfectly is total bullshit.

"Hey show me some respect. I am your superior," he says raising his voice and pointing his finger at me.

"Forget this!" I walk off. Freaking RA solved nothing. Not only was that a complete waste of time but now the RA probably will side with Stanley over everything.

What was that 'superior' crap? That guy thinks that this little power makes him my superior? What does RA stand for to these people? Really Arrogant? I swear the test to get this job has to be like: Do you think you are a god?

There is no winning in my situation. I spend the rest of the semester out of my own dorm room. I only go in to sleep and the rest of the time I stay out. The less I see Stanley the less chance there is of me snapping that dick's neck. It isn't easy staying away. It seems like anywhere I go he goes out of his way to make a presence each day. He knows he has control. If I slip up just a little, he'll tell the RAs that I hit him or something, and they'll believe him. I can't believe a druggie outsmarted me.

The only good thing about being pretty much exiled from my own room is that all the studying for Physics has to take place in Alice's room. Emily is probably the best wingman ever. She talks me up in front of Alice and the moment Alice pays more attention to me than her, she excuses herself from the dorm room, sometimes so quietly that we don't notice. One night, right before the final, we meet up in Alice's room again.

Alice and I sit on her bed and Emily sits at the desk. We quiz ourselves back and forth for a bit and then Emily jumps up from her chair. "Hey, I've got to ask Matt a question. I will be back in a bit." She smiles and leaves. I know that she has nothing to ask Matt. She just wants to make sure Alice keeps me in the room a little longer. It's a little after midnight and Alice is getting tired but still desperately needs to study.

"AH! I am never going to pass this class," she says, covering her face with the book.

"Of course you will," I say trying to comfort her.

"There's just so many terms. Absolute Zero, Malus's Law. It's just so much to remember. I'm a dance major. I don't need to know this."

"It's not so hard." She glares at me. "Okay, it's hard."

"Instead of studying all the terms you should just memorize these," she says pointing at a list on a paper, "and I will memorize these."

"So cheat?"

"Well, more helping each other. That's what they want us to learn isn't it? Team work and stuff?"

"I don't know. I mean, I don't want to get in trouble."

"Aw come on. It's not like we'll get in trouble." Her voice gets soft and she places her hand on my leg. I looked down at her hand on my leg, and then up at her. Her big brown eyes look at me, and all thoughts of objecting leave my mind.

"Okay," I say looking away from her, suddenly bashful.

I don't really know what happened next. We study for a few more hours, more talking about anything other than physics. When I wake up I am still in her bed, my arms wrapped around her waist. I stay there for about an hour not wanting to leave. Leaving now would just negate the whole situation.

"What are you doing here?" she calls out when she wakes up. I don't respond. I want it to seem like I was still sleeping. "Tyler!" she hits me in the chest.

"H-hey," I say in a sleepy tone, rubbing my eyes.

"What are you doing here?"

I think she genuinely doesn't recall how we got in this position. Sadly I don't either, even though I try. "I don't know. It was late. We probably just fell asleep." I smile and wait for her to say something.

Alice smiles and lies back down. Just as I am about to make my move she jumps out of bed. "Crap, I got to get ready." She grabs a towel and her sandals. "Still down to help each other on the final?"

"Yeah." I get out of her bed.

"Great!" She gives me a kiss on the cheek and she heads to the showers and I head back to my dorm.

Feeling pretty pumped I can feel a slight strut in my step. I might not have had sex but hey, I am like one step closer.

"Tyler!" I turn to see Emily running towards me. She stops just short of running into me. She's got a big smile on her face. "Same clothes as last night. Nice." She winks.

"Not exactly, but pretty close."

"Pretty close?"

I tell her as much as I can remember about last night and that we just woke up next to each other.

"Hmm," she pauses and thinks for a bit. "Did you at least ask her out?" Her smile leaves her face but I don't know why.

"No, she had to get ready for something, but gave me a kiss on the cheek."

"Why didn't you ask her out?"

"I didn't really think about it. I was just enjoying the moment too much to think about it I guess."

"Okay you have to ask her out right after the final. Okay?"

"Alright."

"Alright? That confident?" she asks as if confused.

"Yeah. Right after the final I will ask her to coffee."

"No. Dinner." She scrunches her face and folds her arms.

"Okay, dinner."

"I've got to get to my Sociology final. I will see you in class." She gives me a hug and runs off.

During the Physics final I have Alice on my left and Emily on my right. The test was 100 multiple-choice questions. A few times I turn the test page and Alice would give my leg a squeeze to get me to turn the page back. Not wanting to accidently give her the wrong answers I look over at Emily's test a few times to make sure I have the right ones. I only get away with looking at Emily's test a couple times. I don't think Emily is the kind of person willing to help people cheat on tests. She is turned in a way that makes it very difficult to see her answers.

It takes Emily only 45 minutes of the allotted two hours to finish. Alice and I stay there for almost the entire time. I know the first half of the test I do good because I used Emily as a reference, but the last half, well, that is a little more unpredictable.

Alice gets up from her chair and gives me a wink. She hands in her test and leaves. I wait there for a minute after she leaves to make sure the professor doesn't think we were working together. I get up and hand my test in and leave. The professor doesn't even acknowledge I turned in my test. When I get outside I look for Alice. Seeing her in the distance I chase after her.

"Alice!" I called out. She doesn't turn around at first. "Alice," I call out again. This time she turns around.

"Oh, hey," she says. She seems like her mind is somewhere else.

"So you think we did good on the test?" I ask.

"Yeah, probably." She turns to walk to the dorms and I walk with her.

"Yeah, I think we got at least a B. Anyways I was wondering if you wanted to go out sometime?"

She looks at me. I turn to look at her thinking that she is stopping but she continues to walk. Doing a little skip jump to catch up to her she gives me a small glance. "I don't think so."

I feel like I was just hit by a bus. Not from the outside, but the inside out. I feel a cold chill run through my veins. "What?" I say, because it's the only word I can muscle out.

"Sorry I just don't see you like that," she says with no inflection in her voice. It's like talking to someone over text. There is no emotion attached.

"What about last night, and the kiss on the cheek this morning?"

"Well that was more of a friend thing. I've got a boyfriend back home anyway."

"Boyfriend?" I'm in shock. I have known her for over five months and not once has she said anything about a boyfriend. Does she really have one or is she just making up an excuse, I ask myself.

"Yeah, his name is Miggy. He's still in high school but he is trying to get accepted here so we can go to the same place next year." I don't know what I feel more shocked about – the fact that she has a boyfriend, or that she never said anything. "Hey, I got to go. I'll see you around."

She walks away as I just stand like a statue waiting for my brain to process everything. I don't understand what just happened. I grab my cell and text Emily. "She has a boyfriend." Taking a seat at a bench, I wait for Emily's response.

My cell buzzes five minutes later. "I'm sorry," Emily responds.

"Did you know that?" I text back.

"No she never said anything."

"Well that freaking sucks."

"Yeah, well there is always next year," she responds trying to cheer me up.

"Yeah, I guess you're right."

I head back down to the dorms and question every second I hung out with Alice. It felt like I had a chance but as soon as the test was over she changed personalities. I wonder if she was just playing me the entire time. Hanging with me just so she could cheat on the final. Maybe she sat next to me during every test just to cheat.

When I get back to the dorm, the RD and Natalie the RA are standing outside my room. The door is open and Stanley is sitting on the bed on the near brink of tears.

"What's going on?" I ask.

"Sit down," says the RD. I walk in and sit on my bed. "Natalie knocked on your door and Stanley opened it. Upon opening the door she saw a bong. Any drug paraphernalia is against the rules. Having any drugs or drug paraphernalia is cause for eviction."

A huge smile appears on my face. Finally Stanley is getting what he deserves. Wish it would have happened earlier so I can have the dorm to myself but hey the last two days aren't so bad either. "Cool so does that mean he's out of here?"

"You both have to pack up and leave by 8:00 p.m. tonight," Natalie says.

"What? Why would I have to leave if you caught him with drugs?" I say my voice nearly cracking.

"Stanley panicked and showed us your stash of marijuana."

"I don't have any marijuana!"

Natalie holds out a small bag of joints. "These were in your shoe in the closet."

"Well it's not mine. He probably put it in there," I try to reason with these two idiots who seem to be driven to kick me out.

"That's not our problem."

"Are you serious? Between the two of us," I point at me and Stanley, "which one looks like they do drugs?" pointing with force at him, "THE FREAKING STONER!"

"Do not use that tone to me."

"Screw you. You are trying to kick me out because you put me in a room with a freaking stoner and that grounds for kicking me out."

"He was smoking weed, and says that you do drugs too."

"What is wrong with you? I wasn't even here when you busted him. You have no proof."

"If that's the case you should have changed rooms but you didn't. You will have to leave by 8:00 pm tonight or we will have you escorted out by campus police."

My rage builds up. I can feel my face burn bright red as I let out all my anger out on Stanley. With in a second I am off my bed and attacking Stanley. I get in at least seven punches before the RD and RA pull me off. "You're a liar, you asshole!"

The next thing I know I am sitting outside my door with campus police, watching Stanley move his stuff out of the dorm. When he is done it is my turn to try and shove all my stuff in my car. The policeman stands staring down at me with one hand on his taser. Part of me questions if I can get one good slug in before being zapped with a thousand volts of electricity. Stanley grabs his last piece of crap and gives me a slight smile over his tear-stained face. I jump up quickly to attack him again but the policeman catches me and forces me to sit down again. When Stanley is finally out of sight I am let in to my dorm.

I slam each article of clothing in my bag, pretending they're rocks and the bottom of the bag is Stanley's stupid face. The cop just stands at the doorway watching me, his hand still fixed on his taser. It took me six trips to get everything in my car. On the last trip I saw Emily coming back from her final.

"Tyler, what happened?" she asks all concerned.

"Stanley got me kicked out." I throw my bag hard into my car.

"I'm so sorry." She hugs me but I'm so angry I can't hug her back. "You can sleep in my room tonight if you want."

"Thanks..." I start before the cop jumps in.

"No. You are not allowed in campus housing anymore," the cop says.

"I have one more final tomorrow! What am I suppose to do?" I say but he just shrugs.

"Come on. Let's go to the cafeteria and figure this out," Emily says pulling at my arm.

We start walking up to campus. "You have to move your car," says the cop.

"What? Why?" I ask.

"This parking lot is reserved for residents of the dorms, which you are no longer."

Now I want to kick this cop right in his stupid face. "I will meet you at the cafeteria, okay?" Emily says grabbing at my arm again, but this time trying to keep me from charging at the policeman.

"Sure." I get in my car and slam the car door as hard as I can and drive to one parking lot over and park.

Getting up to the cafeteria I see Emily waiting for me. I sit down and nearly knock myself out by slamming my head against the table.

"I am so sorry Tyler," she says.

"Should I just spread my legs and let everyone kick me in the balls?"

"Don't talk like that! You just are having a little bad luck."

"This whole year is bad luck. What the heck did I do to deserve this crap?" I lift my head and push my hands in my eyes. I am near tears but I think my anger is keeping them in my eyes.

"At least this will make a good story when you're older." I just look at her. "So what are you going to do now?"

"About what?" I say throwing my hands up slowly. There is so much I need to figure out it's impossible to know what thing she is talking about.

"You've got one more final tomorrow. Where are you going to sleep?"

"My car I guess." She just looks at me. I know she wants to help but she can't. "What do I tell my parents?"

"You could tell them the truth."

"That my roommate stored drugs in my shoe and that's why I got kicked out of the dorms. They won't believe that. They are the kind of parents who believe guilty until proven innocent."

She pauses for a moment and looks around the cafeteria searching for a solution. "What if you tell them you had a horrible time and you just don't want to go back. Don't tell them you got kicked out."

Emily's got a point. I could just tell them I hated my time there and think I'd do better somewhere other than the dorms. "But what about next year? There is no way they would co-sign on a apartment."

"What about a frat? You could join one of those," she suggests.

"Yeah I could do that, but don't they take in people like the second or third week of the semester? I still need to find a place to live for a few weeks, and there is no guarantee that I will even get into the frat."

"Of course you can get in! They will love you. You just need to make sure not to attack them." She smiles and I smile back, but not for long. "For now I guess you could live in your car, or you could get a job over the summer and just pay for a motel room for the first month.

"I'll have to work all summer to afford something like that."

"Well do you have a better idea?"

"No. I hope I get one though."

She waits for me to calm down more before saying anything else. "Come on I will buy you dinner." She gets up and tugs at my arm to follow her.

"Okay." Emily takes me to get some Mexican food and for a few brief moments I am able to forget the crap storm I'm in.

The next day I wake up in my car again, my back hurting from sleeping sitting up all night. I take my final and drive straight home. When I get home I tell my parents that I hate the dorms and was looking into joining a frat. I am ready for when they ask where I was going to live in the meantime. I told them I would crash at the dorms for a few weeks before rush week. They believe the lie just like Emily thought they would. For the rest of the summer I work at a restaurant. The hours and work suck but I make enough to live in a motel for four weeks.

Chapter 5

Stains. Torn carpet. A strange smell. And I am sure that there are a few rats in the wall. That's what three months working 30 hours a week plus tips as a busser gets you.

Apparently I am not qualified to take people's orders. Seriously? Is it really something that needs a lot of experience to work at a hole-in-the-wall pizza joint? "Hey, you want a large pizza or an extra large pizza?" Oh yeah, so difficult. Definitely need a few years experience, maybe some special training from a trade school.

I have truly loathed this first week of school. The classes are pointless and once again the school screws the students by expecting us to spend over a thousand dollars on books. For example, my Microeconomics textbook cost me $500. If only they had a giant keg party before they screwed us we'd be okay with it. I swear if the teacher makes us read the book for only one chapter I am literally going to chuck the book at his face. I sold my books before I left for summer - $1,750 worth of books. When I sold them back to the school I got $250. Two books they wouldn't take back because they weren't using that book next year. What a scam.

I go on campus and decide to rush Alpha Kappa Alpha. It is the biggest frat and hopefully that improves my chances of getting in. Rush week is just a joke. I go around to all the frats and talk to them. They talk about stupid things like their community service outreach and their presence on campus. Bull. You are here to get drunk and get laid. That's it!

Signing up is easy. Getting in is a different story. Rush week starts the third week of the semester. It seemed very simple to me when I talked to the "brothers" at the booth. Sign up, do a few silly games, get in to the frat. The best thing about AKA is that joining is relatively cheap compared to any other frat. It's also going to be $300 cheaper living there than the dorms.

The first night of Rush Week is by far the greatest time I have had in college so far. They have a party at the frat house. There's music, booze, and girls. All three are the highest quality. Within the first hour I'm making out with this super hot brunette. No idea what her name is or what she even sounds like. She just comes up to me and we start making out. Little surprised though, not that we make out for a while, but that she is so willing to make out with me considering my current headgear.

When the pledges enter the party we have to wear these baby bonnet things. We have a choice between white, blue, and pink. I picked blue. We also have to wear binkies around our necks. Whenever a brother talks to us we have to quickly put the binky in our mouths until they leave. We were not allowed to talk to them in any way. If we do talk to them or lose our binky we are out. Afraid of losing my binky and getting kicked out, I hold it tight in my fist the entire night, unless it's in my mouth.

That Monday morning the bodies of fallen soldiers cover the fraternity floor. Slowly opening my eyes I am greeted by the crack of a large pledge's ass. Nothing like an ass that close to your face to get you moving after a long night of drinking and partying. Sitting up, just feet from where I guess I spent the night, I shut my eyes tight hoping that this hangover would just go away. After maybe an hour of sitting in the middle of the room surrounded by trashed pledges, I get up and head out. Looking at my clock I see the time. 9:45am. Fifteen minutes to get to Econ. Crap.

As soon as I touch the doorknob I hear the worst noise ever. "Pledge! Where are you going?" I turn to see one of the brothers on the stairs looking down at me. He is wearing bright green short shorts and a tank top with the words "Party" on it. Unable to form words I just point at the door hoping he understands what I am getting at. "I don't think so!" he screams. He walks down and grabs hold of my arm pulling me back into the room filled with passed out drunks. I get a small chuckle at the fact that a midget is leading me back to the room. He has to be just over five feet tall. "Listen up!" he screams, but no one moves or shows that they can hear him. "WAKE UP BITCHES!" he screams over and over until everyone wakes up.

"What?" asks one of the pledges.

"WAKE UP!" he screams inches away from the guy's ear. Standing in the middle of the room he lifts his hands as if he just won something. "Congratulations on your first party. Now clean it up!"

"I got to get to class," I say, leaning on the doorframe for stability.

"What!" he says rushing over to me. He stops when we are touching chest to chest, well more chest to stomach.

I'm so tired. Part of me wants to just rest my chin on the top of his head. "I have econ in like ten minutes."

"Not today Pledge. No class for any of you!" He turns back and goes to the center of the room again. "No one is allowed to leave here until this place is spotless! Anyone who leaves will lose their bid." He pauses as he enjoys everyone's groans of frustration. "Get going Bitches!" With that he leaves the room.

Slowly everyone begins to clean except for one guy who is still sleeping on the couch.

I start shaking the guy on the couch and wait for him to open his eyes. "Dude, get up you got to clean."

"No I don't." He rolls over to hide his face.

"You're going to get kicked out dude," I tell him, hoping that will make him get up and help.

"No," he mumbles getting up from the couch and stumbling out the front door.

I am mad that we lost a pair of hands to help clean but I am happy that I have one less guy to compete with for a spot. Four hours of cleaning later and we are finally done. Fearing that we'll get kicked out if we leave without being released we stay in the main room until one of the brothers release us. We wait for two hours, just sitting there completely drained, until one of the brothers walks in.

"You know cleaning the place isn't going to help your chances getting in," he says.

"One of the brothers told us to," one of the guys on the couch says.

"What? Which one?" the brother asks.

"A short one," the guy on the couch makes a gesture with his hand hovering it just a few feet above the ground.

"You mean Chad? Wow, what a dick. No he was a pledge last year. It's first year brother's job to clean up after the parties. We don't make pledges clean unless you make it in." With that the brother goes up the stairs laughing. I can hear the muffled sounds of him screaming something like: "You're a brilliant douchbag Chad!"

The twenty or so pledges do the zombie walk out of the fraternity. I missed all my classes and I'm so tired I can't even drive back to my shithole motel room. As soon as I get into my car I fall asleep. For the first time I actually am happy to fall asleep in my car.

Suddenly my cellphone goes off. "You have 15 minutes to get to AKA or you are out!" a voice screams. I quickly exit my car and run through the cold night air. As I get closer to the frat house I can see a few other pledges running as well. Running into the house I trip on the threshold of the door and eat it hard, rolling into the main room. The only thing that stopped me was the brother I rolled into. I knock his legs right from under him he falls hard on my back. We both scream. Within mere seconds of him landing on me, he quickly stands up and then picks me up by my shirt. At first I thought I was going have that midget Chad giving me crap again but no. The brother standing in front of me is a huge six foot six inch monster of a man. He has blonde hair and is very pale but you wouldn't be able to tell by his red face as he yells at me.

"What is wrong with you!" he screams.

Terrified by the creature in front of me, I look down and back pointing at the door. "I'm sorry I tripped."

"You tripped! You could have broke my leg you little..." at that moment he grabs my shirt with one hand and reached back to punch with the other hand.

"Troy stop!" a voice calls out right before the fist reaches my face. Uncovering my face that was being protected by my hands I see a black guy in a red shirt and black pants. "Let go of him go."

"He nearly broke my leg!" Troy tries to argue.

"Drop," he says to Troy like he is a dog. Troy pushes me back and I nearly fell down again. "First lesson Pledges. We DO NOT hit Troy! He is the starting tight end and we don't want to hurt his draft chances." Troy just snarls at me clenching his fist like at any second he will hear "Hike" and charge me.

"Pledges, you will spend the next five days doing what we say when we say it. If you fail in any way you will lose your bid."

I look around at the pledges. Everyone still looks hungover and one guy is about to fall over.

"Now! First of all," he says walking over to one of the pledges. "Where is your bonnet and binky Pledge?"

"Ahh..." the pledge feels around his head. "It's in my dorm room?" he says terrified.

"And that's how you lose your bid."

"What?" the pledge says.

"Chris, Rick," he says to two brothers behind the pledge, pointing at the bonnet-less pledge. They grab the pledge by the arms and push him out of the frat house. The pledge screams and yells but the other pledges show no reaction to his eviction. At that moment I realize that I am still wearing the bonnet and binky. Luckily I was so hungover that I don't even think of taking them off. "Now pledges. We have 18 of you wannabes rushing. We only have eight openings, and you know what that means? Ten of you are shit out of luck! My name is Chris. When addressing me or any of your other brothers you will address them as 'Brother' followed by their name. So you," he says pointing at the pledge next to me. "I ask, what is your name? You say?"

"Brother Chris, my name is Mitch!" he says quickly.

"Good, but you must also bow your head to the brother. If you don't, well, figure it out. Is that understood?"

"Brother Chris yes!" we all say and bow our heads.

"Good, we got some smart guys here. Now line up in two rows!" Quickly we rush to get in two lines. "Now face the door." Facing the door we all stay frozen, not wanting to upset him. "Grab the hand of the brother next to you." We hold the hand of the pledge next to us and if the clammy feel of the pledge next to me is any indication, there are a lot of scared pledges. "You have now found your pledge buddy. If he doesn't get in you don't get in. You will perform every challenge we have with your pledge buddy. For this one you may not let go of your pledge buddy's hand. To make sure, you will be watched by one of the brothers." Turning around towards his brothers, Chris speaks to them. "Brothers! Who would like to see who fails and who succeeds? I need nine of you to follow the pledges around for tonight's challenge." A few brothers take a step forward. "Stand next to who you'd like to follow."

A cold chill runs through my body. I don't need to turn to see who is standing next to me. "You will fail!" I hear Troy whisper in my ear. I nearly let go of my pledge buddy's hand at the sound of his voice.

"Good. For your first challenge, I'm hungry. I want a burrito, not just any burrito but a Carne Asada burrito with no onions, with mild salsa, and double avocado. I want that exact order. The last pair of pledge buddies to bring me my order loses! Go!"

We all run out as fast as we can out of the frat house. Of course I have the fat guy as my pledge buddy, six-feet tall and about five feet around. "I'm Arnold," he says as we run.

"Tyler," I say back. "This way! My car's over here!" We run and Troy follows. He is purposely running slow, but I don't think he realizes that Arnold is running full speed.

We get to my car. Since our hands are locked together, I am forced to climb over the center to get to the driver side. I turn on the car and start to back up when I see Troy just standing outside looking at me. I roll down the window. "Brother Troy, are you coming?" I ask, not forgetting to bow.

"I want to but someone forgot to open the door for me," he says smiling.

Arnold struggles to get out of the car and then we quickly open the back passenger door for Troy. He just looks at us and shakes his head. We run to the other side and open that door. Once again he shakes his head. Not knowing what to do, I look at him.

"Brother Troy, where would you like to sit?" I ask bowing once again.

Slowly he makes his way over to the front passenger seat and sits down, slowly putting on his seat belt. Now Arnold has to sit in the back, while I drive, and we continue to hold hands. It is even more difficult to get in the car this time and we nearly release our grip. Troy points, thinking that we were about to let go but quickly pushed back in his seat in protest knowing he couldn't blame us for letting go. He could have lied to Chris and said we did but I don't think they are allowed to lie to each other.

Driving is very difficult because of the awkward twist in my arm. When we get to the closest Mexican place there was already a long line and a few pledge buddies already there.

"Go up that way," says Arnold, pointing out of the shopping center.

"What are you talking about?" I ask.

"El Mariachi's is six blocks down, the line might not be so bad there."

For a second I think it's a waste of time but I wouldn't doubt a fat man and food. "Okay," I say as we drive to the next Mexican place.

We get to El Mariachi, after another uncomfortable negotiation through the car. Troy knocks on the window, waiting for us to open the door for him so he can get out.

"Welcome to El Mariachi's. What can I get you?" a woman with a heavy accent asks.

"Carne Asada burrito, no onions, salsa, double avocado," I say.

"Mild salsa!" Arnold quickly says.

"Yeah, mild salsa." I look at him and give him a nod for the catch.

"$10.25," the woman says.

"And I will have two flautas," says Troy. We turn and look at him as he just gives us a wink.

"Is that all together," she asks.

"Yes, please hurry," I say.

"$17.75"

We nervously wait for the order right at the counter. As soon as she hands us the order we grab it and make a dash to the car with Troy slowly walking behind. Arnold opens the door for Troy and he sits down.

"My order?" asks Troy. I had him the bag and he quickly hands it back. "I just want mine." I take the bag and put it on the ground as I take out his flautas and hand it to him. "Good."

Again we awkwardly get in the car and drive to back to the frat. The drive back, Troy eats his flautas in the messiest way possible making sure to get more food all over my car than in his mouth. We run as fast as we can back to the house. It's about a ten minute run that I could have made in five if I didn't have Arnold running with me. On the way we are passed by four groups of pledges. In my head I think, if we lose because of Arnold I may just punch him in the head. Troy is keeping up with us but just because he needs to make sure we continue to hold hands.

We get to the house and there are already all the other pledges there. "Shit," I scream. I try to let go of Arnold's hand but he won't let go of me. I glare at him to let go of my hand but he doesn't.

"Not over yet," say Arnold.

"Goodbye asshole," says Troy as he passes.

"What are you two still doing here?" say Chris as he walks over to Arnold and me.

"B-brother Chris ah..." says Arnold as he stutters through his words. "They might have gotten your order wrong." He finishes with a bow. I bow as well as he looks at me.

"Tubby's right," says Chris as he walks in the center of the room. "Line up!" We quickly line up. Slowly Chris opens each bag and grabs out the burrito taking one large bite. The first three are right. With each bite my hand shakes more and more. Six of the pledge buddies have gotten the order right. On the seventh Chris takes a bite. "Ah! Onions! You morons!" screams Chris throwing the burrito on the ground. "Get out now! You two will not be AKAs!" The two ejected pledges walk out yelling at each other. I don't hear as I am too excited by Arnold's foresight. "Don't get too happy Pledge, you might have gotten the order wrong too.

The guys next to us get their order right and I begin to shake as he grabs our burrito. We didn't check it! What if we ordered it right and the idiots got the order wrong? We could still be wrong and get kicked out.

Chris takes a big bite. "This is the worst burrito I have ever hand." He spits the burrito on the floor and I can feel it land on my shoe. "But the order's right." We let out a big breath of relief as I hear Troy scream and then the sound of something hitting the wall hard. I think he kicked the wall realizing we passed the first test. "Okay, walk your pledge buddy home and we will see you tomorrow. You won't be followed but we expect you to continue to hold hands. Good night."

With that I walk Arnold back to the dorms where he lives joking about how we nearly got kicked out and then make my way back to the crap hole motel.

The next day we get a text to meet at the frat house at 10:00 pm. I meet Arnold at the parking lot and we walked over together holding hands to the frat house. We get to the frat house and walk in.

"What the hell dudes," say one of the brothers, the same brother that told us of Chad's deception.

"Brother..." I pause.

"Todd," he says.

"Brother Todd, aren't we suppose to hold hands?" I say with a bow.

"Dude that was just the first challenge." He points to the other pledges not holding hands. Quickly Arnold and I let go and wipe our hands on our shirts.

We wait until midnight for Chris to tell us our challenge. Finally Chris comes down the stairs and walks to the center of the room.

"Grades come first boys. Well at least for me, not for you," he says. He must have been doing homework as we were forced to wait. "Line up!" he screams and we quickly stand in a straight line. "For tonight's challenge you will rely on your pledge buddy to get you through. Decide who will be responsible for your success or failure.

I look at Arnold. "I'll do it," I say. Arnold gives me a nod. I think he knows that if we are going to win any challenge, we'll have the best shot if I take charge. If he does, and they decide to have us run a mile, he may die.

"Time's up! Who have you chosen to do the challenge?" Eight of us raise our hands. "Okay, sit over here." He points to two couches and we awkwardly sit on the couch all smashed together. "Your challenge tonight," he says looking at us, "is to watch your pledge buddy save your ass!" He quickly turns and points to the other eight on the other side of the room. My heart drops as I fear we have been tricked into losing. "Brother Chad, please bring me the hat of fate." Chad walks over and hands Chris a goofy big stripe hat. Chris puts his hand in the hat and starts pulling out little pieces of scrap paper. "In here are pieces of paper with challenges. There is everything from bringing a girl back to the frat house, to the last man standing challenge. That's when we have you run around the house until someone quits." He stops and looks at Arnold. "Brother Troy, will you do the honors."

Troy reaches in and looks at me as he grinds his teeth. I know he wants the last man standing paper. He pulls out a piece of paper and hands it to Chris.

"Oh!" he says looking around at his brothers. "DODGE BALL!" With those words the brothers scream with a mighty roar. I think we are dead. Arnold is not nimble and he is close to three times as wide as the rest of the guys. "For this challenge the brothers will throw volleyballs at you. First one to call it quits, he and his pledge buddy are out. If you fall, you have three seconds to get up. Stand at the wall."

The eight stand at the wall as one of the brothers brings out two bags of volleyballs. The brothers all reach in for a ball and I watch as Troy focuses on Arnold. Clearly Arnold will be the main target. One of the pledges turns around. "No Bitch," yells Chad. "Face forward."

"Brothers ready?" say Chris.
"Ready!" they all scream.
"GO!"

With that they all begin to attack the helpless pledges with volleyballs. I watch as Arnold is hit three times more then anyone else. He is wearing down. I can see him slowly melt down as the volleyballs begin to take toll on his body.

Suddenly, I see the pledge next to Arnold get hit hard in the balls. He falls over screaming. He tries to get up but gets hit right in the face. A big red mark appears instantly on his face. "No more!" he screams.

"And we got a pansy!" screams Chris as the balls stop flying. "You and your pledge buddy are out!"

The two ejected pledges walk out. I look out the front door and watch them begin to argue. Suddenly the one who sat on the couch cocks back his fist and plants it straight on his buddy's face. He walks away as his buddy slowly gets up.

Chris waits for a bit as the victims slowly stabilize themselves. "See you tomorrow."

I walk out with Arnold. "Dude, great job!" I say, so excited that he survived I give him a huge hug.

"Ah!" he screams. "Don't touch."

"Sorry dude," I laugh.

"We better get in after this crap."

"We will, Arnold, we will. I'll catch you tomorrow."

The third night they kind of take it easy on us. Not wanting to cause anymore visible bruises, we just have to play a game. Trivia to be precise. Five hours of trivia. Topics from sports to the brothers' favorite foods. After the five hours the losers get kicked out. When it was other people's turns I can see Troy mouth the answers. Sometimes they got it from his help and sometimes they just couldn't figure it out.

After the five hours the game ends. The scores are tallied and we got fourth. Just survived.

Thursday I meet Emily at the cafeteria and tell her all that is happening with rush week.

"Wow, you owe Arnold, don't you?" said Emily.

"What do you mean?" I asked, confused.

"Well, if he didn't know the other Mexican place, and withstand all the volleyballs, you'd be out. Do you really think you could have lasted that long getting hit?"

I think about it for a bit. No I couldn't have. I would have probably given up in half the time.

"Shit!" I say under my breath.

"What?" she says all concern.

"Troy's coming."

"Oh, the jerk who hates you?"

"Yeah."

Troy walks over and stands looking at me like he wants to punch me in the face. I look up slowly at him. He spends just a second looking at me eye to eye before he notices Emily at the other side of the table.

"Who's this?" ask Troy.

"Brother Troy, this is Emily," I say giving a small bow of the head.

"Hey cutie, I'm Troy Tompkins. Tight End." He gives her a wink and I dig my nails into my leg under the table.

"Hi," she says back, unimpressed.

"You two dating?" asks Troy.

"Brother Troy, no," I say with a bow.

"Hmm," he pauses as he strokes either side of his chin. "How about we go out sometime?"

My heart stops. He just asked Emily out. Could she actually say yes? I don't want her to date this dick, but if she says no he might take it out on me.

"What were you thinking," she asks.

"Dinner, maybe a walk on the beach?" he says.

"That sounds fun." My jaw nearly drops off its hinges. "I have a big paper due Monday though. You will have to ask me again Tuesday," she says giving him a wink and flipping her hair a little.

"Alright," says Troy. My body cringes at his arrogance. "Can I get your number so I can call you Tuesday?"

"Yeah!" she grabs his hand and writes her number on it.

"Talk to you later girl," he says as he walks away, giving her a final wink.

"Bye Troy," she responds giving him a tiny wave.

I just stare stunned. "What the..." I start but not knowing how to finish.

"Please," she says taking a drink of water. "Like I'd date that tool. You find out if you are in Saturday right?"

"Yeah," I say, still confused.

"Well if he knows we are friends he should take it easy on you. I mean, if he wants a date from this 'cutie' next week." She gives me a sarcastic wink.

"You are a genius."

"Don't I know it."

That night at the frat house I learn she was right. Troy doesn't seem so bitter towards me. Instead of snarling he actually smiles at me. I think Emily saved my ass.

"Helloooo pledges!" says Chris. "I got a test tomorrow so you get to have another easy night of challenges." It feels like a small weight is taken off my chest. "Tonight all you have to do is bring a girl to the diner across from campus. Oh, and the girl isn't for you. It is for your brother!" Troy gives me a smile. "If you bring a girl, your brother will give you this green pass." He holds out a green piece of paper in the air. "You can then go home and we will see you tomorrow. Brothers, find your pledges and tell them what you like in a girl. Good night."

I watch as Chris goes up the stairs. As I turn I have Troy just inches away from me. Looking up I see him smiling down at me.

"Brother Troy, what kind of girl do you like?" I ask afraid of what he will say.

He smiles at me like a creeper. "You know," he whispers. Then he just walks away.

"What is that supposed to mean?" asks Arnold.

"It means I am about to call in one freaking huge favor," I say, walking out of the frat house.

I pull out my cell to call Emily.

"Who you calling?"

"A friend," I tell Arnold.

"Hey, Tyler. Did they wax your head or something tonight?"

"No...ah here's the thing. The challenge tonight is to get a girl to the diner across the street."

"Oh, gotcha. I will be there in like ten minutes," she says cheerfully.

"Well not exactly."

"What do you mean?"

I pause for a bit as I think of the best way to say this. "We have to find a girl for one of our brothers."

"What are you saying?" I can hear her voice change, as she is about to get angry.

"Arnold and me have to bring you to have a dinner date with Troy. If we don't we are out."

"What the hell Tyler," she screams so loud I have to take the phone away from my ear. "There is no way that I am going on a date with that tool."

"I know! I'm sorry! I don't want to ask you this. It's just, if you don't, Arnold and I are kicked out and I will have to drop out of school.

"Screw you!" she says letting out a deep breath and hanging up.

I drop my phone from my ear and stick in back in my pocket. "So..." says Arnold.

"I don't know."

The two of us go to the diner and watch as the pledges bring girl after girl to the brothers. An hour goes by and we are the only two who haven't brought a girl for their respective brother. Slowly Troy's anticipation turns to anger. He gets up from the booth he has been sitting at for over an hour and walks over to us.

Pulling out the green card he rips it in front of my face. "You're out asshole."

"Hey!" The three of us turn to see Emily running in the diner. "Sorry I'm late I was up north today. Hi Troy," she wraps her arm around his.

"Congrats," says Troy as he hands us both halves of the torn green card. "I will see you two tomorrow." He winks and looks down at Emily. I nod, and hope that Emily realizes how thankful I am. "Hey, Tyler," he yells at me as I'm reaching the door. "Tomorrow should be interesting."

"That was close man," says Arnold.

I pause for a moment. "Sorry, I just...I don't know what he is going to try with her."

"You like her or something?"

"No. She's just a really good friend." I look back at the diner, seeing the two laugh and carry on.

"Really?" he pauses. "She's a good friend?"

The next day I try calling and texting Emily a hundred times but she never answers. Is she afraid that I am going to ask her for another favor, or is she mad at me and never wants to talk to me again, or what if she had a great time and went home with Troy last night? The more I think about it, the more I begin to panic.

At the frat house we sit again for hours, silently waiting for Chris to give us orders.

"Line up!" yells Chris. We quickly line up. "Fourteen left. Six will not make it. Last night! This is when we decide who is worthy of becoming a brother, and who is a wannabe." He walks around looking at us individually. "You should be happy you made it this far. I'm surprised some of you made it this far." He looks directly at Arnold. "You shouldn't be proud that you made it this far just to lose though. Tonight you will run the gauntlet. If you and your pledge buddy fail to complete the gauntlet you are out! Brothers stand behind the pledges."

The brothers walk behind us. I can feel Troy is right behind me. He is close enough that I can feel his breath on the back of my neck.

"To complete this task you will be punished. We will take all weakness from you. If you can survive this 60 minute challenge you will be an AKA. You will run to five stations around the frat house. Station one you will be pepper sprayed. Station two takes you to station three. This path is covered with sharp rocks. Take off your shoes and socks." We take off our shoes and socks. Arnold has trouble taking them off as fast as the others. "Station three you will eat three jalapeño peppers. Station four you will be punched in the gut 30 times. Finally you will go to station five where the brother behind you will paddle you five times. When you finish, you repeat the process. If you stop at any time you are out. Brothers take your positions! Pledges prepare to be sprayed. Any final questions?"

"If we all keep going does that mean we all get in?" ask Arnold.

"No, if you all survive it will be up to your brother if you and your pledge buddy join the frat," responds Chris.

Troy grabs my shoulder and gets close to my ear. "Your friend rejected me." I swallow some spit. He is going to kill me. If at least three people don't quit Arnold and me are out.

"Brothers ready!" screams Chris.

"Ready!" they scream around the house. I can hear Troy's voice louder then them all. "Go!"

Seconds after Chris calls for the start we are sprayed with pepper spray for ten seconds. The screams are loud as everyone's eyes feel like they are on fire. Struggling to find the next station, I feel a push by one of the brothers. For a second I think they want me to succeed, but no, they just want to watch me burn more.

I get to the rock path and I can feel my feet get cut up. I fall a few times and struggle to get up but the screams of the brother yelling at me to continue get me moving. As I get past station two I can feel something wet under my feet. At first I think its oil they put on the ground, but then I figure out its just my blood. The spray is destroying my eyes. My vision is so blurry I can't tell where anyone is or if anyone has given up. I get pushed to station three and am handed the jalapeño peppers. Trying to get through it quickly all at once I put them all in my mouth and try to do it in one bite. Fifteen agonizing bites later I swallow them. I gasp for a cool breath but breathing has now become painful. I hold my breath as long as I can but have to take a breath to not pass out and it's the worst pain ever! I reach station four. The only reason I know I got there is because I start getting punched like crazy. They are supposed to hit us in the gut but a few times I feel my ribs getting attacked. I don't know if they count or just estimate the punches. Either way it felt more than 30. Slowly I hobble over to station five. As soon as I get there I feel Troy's massive paws grab me and push against the wall. Slowly he reaches back and slams that paddle on my ass. I let out loud screams and he laughs. One...two...three...four...five.

"Next station Pledge!" yells Troy.

Three times I have to repeat the gauntlet. I don't know where anyone else is. Everything is a big blur. I keep my eyes closed most of the time. The brothers push me to the next station anyways. It's better that they push me around than I struggle to see where I am. At least with my eyes closed I have some relief.

"Finish off the station you're on!" yelled Chris.

Whatever station we are on would be our last. I was in so much pain that I am just happy to be done. "I get you last Bitch!" My last station, Troy.

"One!"   I   said   slowly. "Two...Three...Four...Five!"

Snap!

I fall to the group screaming in pain as I hear the brothers around me screaming and two of them are holding me down so I don't move.

"He moved...it's not my fault!" I hear Troy say. There's fear in his voice.

There is a splash of something in my eyes. Some of it runs down my face and into my mouth. They are trying to use milk to clear up my eyes.

"What are we going to do Chris!" someone screams.

"Just let me think! Just get him cleaned up!" says Chris. I can see. Well, my eyes are still blurry but I can see. "Get everything cleaned up now! Hey, Tyler you okay? Can you hear me?"

"My leg, it hurts." I look down. It's bent the wrong way. "What happened?"

"The paddle slipped and your leg broke. It's going to be okay. We are going to get you an ambulance."

"When will it be here?" I begin to tremble.

"We haven't called them yet," say Chris.

"Why the hell not!" I scream.

Chris pauses until I stop yelling. "If we call the ambulance and you tell them what happened we are all screwed. No more AKA you got that?"

"Call the damn ambulance!" I scream.

"Listen! Listen! You need to tell them you tried to jump over the railing and you leg snapped. You do that you're in the frat and we all get to stay."

"What? No!"

"Listen if you don't we are all done. We all get kicked out. Please!" I can hear the desperation. "You will be an AKA and you will never be required to clean or do anything. We will pay for your beer and we will owe you one."

I pause and bite my tongue. The brothers wait for me to speak. "We all get in," I say.

"What?" asks Chris.

"Everyone makes the frat."

"Okay," say Chris as he become more relieved.

"Now call the damn ambulance!" I scream.

"Someone call 911, we need to move him towards the stairs!"

Four people slowly pick me up as I feel my leg dangle. They put me down by the stairs and I scream uncontrollably until the ambulance comes, a moment of relief as the give me some morphine for the pain.

I spend the night in the hospital. I can't recall much of what happened between the frat and the hospital bed I lay in now. My leg is wrapped from just under my knee to my toe. When I wake up only Arnold is in my room.

"Arnold!" I say. He's sleeping. "Arnold!" I turn just enough that a shot of pain goes through my body. My scream wakes him.

"Hey Tyler. How you feeling?"

"My leg freaking hurts!"

"Yeah, it was a pretty nasty break. The good news is you're in the frat," he says trying to cheer me up. "They guys checked you out of the motel you were at and moved your stuff in the frat house." I don't respond. "Doctor said you could go home tonight if you want. You have to have the cast on for five weeks and then stay of crutches for like two months."

"Anyone call my parents?"

"No, the brothers said it would be better if you called them."

"They are going to be freaking pissed."

I call my parents and they are pissed but they can't do anything to punish me so they just take turns yelling at me. Arnold stays with me and then drives me to the frat house. With my right leg wrapped up it looks like I won't be doing anymore driving. In the car I just look out the window.

"Thanks by the way," say Arnold breaking the silence.

"Thanks for what?"

"You got me in the frat." I look over as the big smile on his face. "I didn't make it through the gauntlet. I got sprayed and then walked over those rocks and I couldn't take it anymore so I had to give up. I'm sorry but I just couldn't."

"Did anyone else give up?" I ask.

"Yeah, almost everyone. Only you and three other guys were able to survive the entire time."

"Great."

"I know!" Arnold didn't get the sarcasm.

The rest of the drive is silent. Slowly I crutch my way to the frat house door. I am slow but at the perfect pace for Arnold. When we get to the frat I am looked at like a leper. Like if any of the brothers touched me, they too would have their legs broken.

"You're on the third floor," says Arnold.

"Seriously," I say quietly. It takes five minutes of slowly hopping to get to my room. It's a small two-person room.

"I got to go finish a paper. You okay?"

"Yeah I'm good."

"Okay, I'm two doors down on the left. Thanks again Tyler." He walks out and I just fall on my premade bed. At least the guys got my room put together.

I just lay in my bed looking up at the ceiling waiting until I can take another Vicodin. The door is kicked open and I jerk up, the jerk causing an excruciating spasm in my leg. There in the doorway was a familiar face, the tool on the couch that refused to help clean the house with us.

"I got you in too?" I ask.

He looks at me for a bit and then speaks. "My dad and his dad got me in." He throws his bag on his bed. Taking off his shirt he moves the closet door over and pulls out a clean one. He looks at me with an arrogant smile. "Legacy, Bitch. I don't rush. I just get in. Later cripple." With that he slams the door behind him as he leaves.

I swear into the pillow for a good five minutes. Another dick roommate.

Chapter 6

Have you ever felt like you were trapped? Not in the sense of being trapped in a cage, but trapped outside of the cage. That's how I feel. I feel trapped on the outside. Fraternity life is nothing I expected it to be. Then again, I didn't expect to have my leg in a cast and have to take Vicodin so I don't cry every second. Parties are a joke. I'm not supposed to drink while I take the pills but I usually have one beer. If I wasn't on the pills I'd feel the same way, but now I only need to have one beer to be dizzy and slightly confused rather than ten. It's funny. I thought that having a cast on my leg would give me the sympathy play with the girls. A couple dozen girls have signed the cast but they only stay long enough to ask what happened and sign the cast.

Two minute later they are off trying to have a drunken one-night stand with one of the other frat guys.

   The frat guys all stay away from me. They say hello but have no intention of hanging out or talking other then basic salutations. One guy, Greg, he talks to me but that's only when he walks with me to my Econ class. Hell, the only reason he does that is because he knows I am slow getting there on my crutches. I usually show up late but the teacher for that class doesn't care. I don't know if it's because he understands it's difficult for me to get around, or that he genuinely doesn't care that I am there. When Greg and I walk to class, he usually just puts on his headphones and walks next to me. As soon as we get to the class he grabs my backpack off my shoulders and holds the door open for me. I think he purposely makes sure he opens the door in such a way that everyone in there is startled by the noise. He always apologizes to the teacher, then walks over with me to my seat, drop off my backpack, and then sits next to this girl in the class he probably is trying to get with. He plays the good guy card perfectly in front of his audience. I'm always tempted to tell Greg to stop using me, but he is the closest thing I have to a friend in that frat next to Arnold.

   Arnold. My broken leg might put off girls, but it will get better in like three weeks. Arnold will always be fat. The guy is huge. If he was to meet a girl he'd kill her in bed. I'm not trying to be mean but its true. I don't know if he could have sex if he wanted to. I think it's physically impossible. That's the thing though, he's a great guy, and I think he's smart. I don't know for sure but I've never seen him bummed out about papers or tests. He is probably the third least popular person in the frat but it still puts him a spot ahead of me and two steps ahead of my roommate Trevor Hackley. Worst thing is he refuses to answer to Trevor. Instead he will only answer to Hack. One time I was trying to get him to turn down his music, or at least put on some headphones, and, like a child, he refused to acknowledge that I was speaking to him. After a dozen times yelling at him I finally called him Hack and he put on headphones. Even then I could hear the music blasting.

I'm lucky when I get a chance to be in my room. The frat has a policy that we all have to follow. If a brother brings a girl back to his room the roommate has two choices. One, leave the room for the rest of the night, or two, cover your face with the blanket and do not remove it. I always pick number one. I don't understand how Hack gets girls to sleep with him. He is such a dick and yet these girls come back here. He is either paying them or he finds the dumbest girls in the world.

Being stationary these last six weeks has been difficult. The only good thing that came from my leg getting broken, besides getting in the frat, is that Emily is speaking to me again. Arnold, once again, is credited for saving my butt. When I got to the hospital he figured while he waited for me to wake up, he'd give her a call. Brilliantly, he called from his phone. If he used mine I wager she wouldn't have answered and not even bothered checking the voicemail. He told her what happened and like a snap of the fingers she was no longer mad at me and acted like I never asked her to meet Troy for a date.

Emily and I hang out a lot now, but she refuses to come anywhere near the frat. She says it's because fraternity and sorority life is just an excuse to get drunk and make random hookups. I think it's because she doesn't want to see Troy. I'm okay with that. If she did see Troy he'd be his typical tool self again and hit on her. Five seconds later and she would not be talking to me again.

I meet Emily outside the Social Sciences building today. We usually meet up at noon every Tuesday. It's a time we both have a break between classes. It's a short break, you know, one of those, 'I got time for a conversation but not too long.' Keeps it simple and usually prevents me from talking about my frat life. Whenever I bring up Hack or the other guys her face gets scrunched up liked she tastes something sour. Arnold is the only exception to that rule but truthfully, he rarely comes up.

"So in Econ the teacher is having us do these web entries. At first I was like sweet, get a group of people together and work on them and we all pass. But since there are only ten questions a class, no one wants to make the time to just meet and do it. They'd rather just do them really quick. It's stupid cause most people get 6 out of 10."

"Yeah," she says looking out into the distance. She doesn't seem too interested in what I'm saying but I continue, not sure what's weighing on her mind.

"Like, come on, if we all get together I bet we could ace them. We have to take 16 of them. Those points add up quickly."

"Yeah," she responds.

"I bet the professor has us do them 'cause it means less work for him. I bet he doesn't even make the quizzes. He just uses someone else's quizzes. That's why most of us fail them, cause he doesn't even teach the same stuff."

"Uh-huh," she says biting the side of her lip.

This time I catch on that she's not paying attention to me. "You know I been thinking that I would make a good dictator."

"Yeah..."

"Most dictators get in by starting a rebellion and killing off the current political leader. So here's the plan. We start a small militia and attack Canada. I figure it will take like fifteen of us to do it. Just have to make sure we take out their moose cavalry. What do you think?" I turn and wait.

She snaps out of her trance and looks at me. "Yeah...of course."

I close my eyes half way and glare for a second. "You think it's a good idea to attack Canada with fifteen people?"

"What?" she shuffles in her seat and puts her hair behind her ear. "No...ahh."

"What's going on with you Emily?" I ask.

"Nothing. Just thinking." She looks away.

"Well, if you are thinking about it, it's not nothing."

"I don't really want to talk about it."

"Emily," I put my hand on her shoulder. "What is it?" She doesn't answer again. I reach down and rub my cast. "Ahh, the pain, it hurts so bad. Would you like to hear about all the things that it's difficult to do with a cast." She rolls her eyes and I know she is close to telling me. "One, showering. I have to wear this bag around it and sometimes I don't even want to shower cause this thing smells so bad. I'm pretty sure I dropped a fry down there and there is a rat living in there looking for the fry. Wouldn't it be freaky if they opened the cast and there is a hug fat rat living in there off the food that drops in the cast."

"Gross, stop!" she screams, giving me a hit across the chest to make sure I stop. "Fine," pausing for a moment. "That guy asked me out again."

This is the first time I ever heard of her getting asked out. I know it probably happens all the time, but since she said "again," I feel like I should have known about it. "And?" I ask.

"And I don't know."

"What did you tell him?"

"I said maybe, but last time I said no so I feel like if he asks again I will say yes." She becomes very irritated at the fact that she wouldn't be able to say no if he asked again.

"Do you like the guy?"

"I don't know," she says as if I should have already known the answer.

"Well, why don't you just go out with him?"

"Why would I do that," she looks at me with disgust.

"One, you are thinking about it. If you didn't want to date him you'd just blow him off and not think of it again. Two, you could always just go out with him once. If he turns out to be a good guy, you go out with him again. If he sucks, then you can just say you don't like him like that and that's it." I stop and wait for her to answer. She scratches he head a bit and tries to speak twice but stops herself before any words escape. "Hey, worst case scenario, you get a free meal," I joke, but I think she thinks I'm serious.

She grabs her backpack and stands up quickly. "I've got to get to class, I'll talk to you later." She hurries away before I can say bye back. Even if I did she wouldn't have heard me probably. Too many voices in her head.

I finish my classes for the day and head back to the frat. The end of the day is my favorite because I can take my Vicodin. The first week I took the pills when I had pain. Sadly I took too many during the school day and, well, I took a Business Ethics test, but I didn't know I took it until I got the test back. I got a D. Fricking sucks, I am actually good in that class. Getting to my room I open my desk drawer and take a pill. My last pill in the bottle. Fifteen minutes from now a lot of pain will leave my body. Knowing I need more pills, I call up the pharmacy.

"I need a refill on a prescription," I tell the pharmacist.

"Sorry, Mr. Freed but you don't have anymore refills," she tells me.

"What, that can't be. I don't get the cast off for another two weeks and I still have pain." I try to reason with her.

"I'm sorry but your original prescription was to last you until you get the cast off. You should have managed your pill intake better." With that the pharmacist hangs up on me.

Two weeks without Vicodin. I could use regular Advil but I'm still going to be in freaking pain the entire time. I quickly go into withdrawal as I struggle to sleep through the night. At most I get an hour of interrupted sleep.

That Friday I sit in bed doing homework trying not to think about the pain. It feels like someone is stabbing me with a large needle. My nerves spasm every once in a while and my leg twitches, making me moan in pain. When the spasms do come I find the best way to deal with the pain is to count down from ten. Even though it takes me 30 seconds to count those ten seconds it seems to help.

"Hey, you got to make yourself scarce again tonight," says Hack as he bursts into the room. "I got this girl coming over, Trish. You know, the Asian girl I brought over like three times. Ahh, girl's amazing!" he says shaking his fists and looking up to the sky.

"Dude, just go to her place," I plead.

"Nah, her roommate's a real bitch."

"Think you two'd get along."

"You'd think." He doesn't get the sarcasm.

"Dude my leg's killing me I need to sleep in my bed."

He pulls his head out of his closet and points at me with a hanger. "Just take one of your pills and you will be fine."

"I can't I'm out."

"Well, go get some more."

"I can't get anymore."

"Really," he turns and I can see some honest sympathy on his face. "Damn, those things were good."

My eyes widen. "What do you mean?"

"They go great with vodka. I pop one of those with a shot and I got this great trip. It was like X without the shakes."

"You were stealing my freaking pills?" I scream.

"Dude, I just took a couple. Settle down."

"Settle down...you asshole! I'm in freaking pain and your stealing my freaking pills! What the hell is wrong with you?"

"You are blowing this way out of proportion dude. Calm down, I just took a few. Hell, the pain is probably in your head."

"What is wrong with you?"

"What's wrong with me? What's wrong with you? Your parents never teach you to share?"

I am stunned, as he doesn't seem to comprehend the agony he has subjected me too. "You know what, screw you dude, just make sure you are out of here tonight. Later asshole," he flips me off and slams the door behind him.

I grab hold of my pillow and scream every word that makes me feel better, and then curse Hack's entire life.

I try to stand to walk it off not realizing I am still in the cast. My rage seems to be the perfect pain reliever as only my brain seems to be on fire. Walking over to his bed I pound the bed as hard as I can as I imagine him under my fists. Slowly stopping something catches my eye. His drawer is slightly cracked and something gold is visible.

I hop around the bed and open the drawer, and there I see these shiny gold objects. Condoms.

Hack is such a tool. I remember the first week he and I lived in the frat. He opened up a dozen boxes of condoms and dumped them into his drawer, telling me his goal was to use every single one. At first I thought he was joking, but after the not being able to sleep in my own bed for four of the first seven days I realize it wasn't a joke.

I held a single condom in my hand studying it, and then looking over at the window. Just throw them out and ruin his whole night. No, I can't do that. If I do that he will just go to one of the other brothers and get one.

I throw the condom back in the drawer slamming it closed and sit on his bed looking at his poster of some blonde bimbo on a motorcycle. The poster became hypnotizing as I see how I can get my revenge. It isn't the girl who gets my attention but the pushpin that holds the poster on the wall.

Pulling the pin out of the wall, the right corner of the poster falls and covers the bimbo's face. Looking at the pin and back at the wall and back to the pin, and then the drawer I feel a sudden shot of excitement. I hobble back to his bed, falling on it. Opening the drawer again I pulled out a single condom and hold it just inches away from the pin.

"I can't," I say quietly to myself. Suddenly my leg spazzes and a shot of pain runs through my body nearly sending me to my back. I moan and before the pain has stopped, I pushed the pin through the condom. Just the action of pushing that pin in the condom relieved some of the pain. I continued to poke holes in all his condoms until the pain was gone. Surprisingly the pain stopped with three holes in the final condom.

That night I take my pillow and blanket and sleep in Arnold's room. Arnold's roommate is lucky.

Never has to worry about not sleeping in his bed. I go past my room and hear the noises of a plan in motion.

I don't talk to Hack for a week. It was a great week. I go to bed around midnight and he shows up after and just goes to bed. He makes the noises of getting ready for bed but that's it. I think him and his girl had a falling out or something 'cause I haven't seen her around.

Arnold drives me to the hospital to get my cast off. For the first time since we had to drive to the final frat challenge I ride in my car. Arnold can barely fit in the driver's seat, but I want to be able to drive my car home from the hospital, and his beat up Toyota is a deathtrap. The car doesn't start at the first turn of the key but on the second it works. Shouldn't have had it sit idle all that time, but I had other things to think of, like pain.

"I met this girl," says Arnold. I just look at him with a crooked smile. I don't know if he has a chance with the girl, but it's nice to hear that he likes one. "She is in my art class I'm taking."

"What's she look like?" I ask.

"Long black hair, blue eyes, and a great body."

As soon as he says "great body" I know he doesn't have a chance, but it's good he gets practicing girls out. "So you going to ask her out or something?"

"What? No I was talking about her for you. Did you hear me say I know a girl for you?" He looks at me for a brief second and then looks back at the road as we turn into the hospital parking lot.

"I must have missed that part, but can you blame me? I got other things on my mind."

"Anyways I think this girl be good for you. Her name's Becky."

"Becky? That doesn't sound very hot."

"Hey, the worse the name, the better the girl," he gives me a wink. "So you want me to introduce you?"

I don't want to offend Arnold but I don't trust his judgment in girls. To me, the better looking the person, the higher the standards. Arnold's a great guy but I think his standards are a lot lower than mine. "Nah dude, maybe in a bit but I just want to get this cast off and relax for a bit. Do some partying."

"Alright, but let me know and I will introduce you."

I give him a chuckle. "Okay dude."

When the cast comes off I feel like my chain of loneliness has fallen off. I still have to walk with a cane but at least my armpits won't be tortured anymore.

We drive back to the school and I go to my Intro to Business class. I feared that class because today is the day we get back our tests. I struggled during that test and the pain from my leg was really bothering me that day. I had already planned to go up to the teacher after class to beg her to give me a second shot because I was distracted by the pain, maybe get an extra credit assignment. When I get my test back, I get a 92%! At first I think it's a mistake, but there was my name on that scantron. A let out a "Booyea" and the whole class looks at me. I don't care. I aced it.

When I get back to the frat house I go up the stairs, making sure to take the steps two at a time because I can. Going to the third floor isn't as much torture as it used to be. As soon as I get to my room I take the scantron and pin it against the wall above my desk. If I had a fridge I would have put it on there. For the first time, I have pride in my accomplishment. Hopping into bed, I just take it easy as I look at that 92% across the room.

The door opens and Hack walks in. Suddenly my happy day feels like a cloud is here to rain on it. I give him a quick look and then go back to staring at the 92%, but I have to take a second look. Usually he has an arrogant smile or a toolish calm expression on his face, but this time he has a troubled look on his face. I don't care but it's like someone else is controlling my mouth.

"What's wrong Hack?" I ask, but I don't really care.

He walks over to his closet and slides open the door and then reaches under his bed and pulled out his suitcase. A suitcase? Was he going on a trip? Was I getting a weekend with him out of my hair? That would be amazing. "I'm leaving," he said sadly, as if his dad just died.

"Why?" I can barely hide my excitement, having to cover my smile with my arm.

"Trish is pregnant." Hack could see the confusion on my face. "The Asian I brought here a couple times."

I had never seen Trish, only heard her from the other side of the door. "Yeah, I remember."

"We had a scare about a week ago, and she told me that she just read the test wrong but she went to the doctor a couple days ago and they confirmed she's pregnant." He stops and sits on his bed, his back turned to me. "My freaking life is over. I had like two more years of sex with as many girls as I want. I had a buffet out here and now I am stuck with Asian for the rest of my life." He starts to cry and I almost bust out laughing.

I get up and pat him on the back. I have a huge smile across my face but he can't see it. I walk towards the door using my cane for support. "I'll give you some time alone." Closing the door slowly, I pump my fist a dozen times. Walking down the hall I start whistling "Hey Hey Hey Goodbye." That would be the last time I would see Hack. He packed up his stuff and headed back to wherever he came from. Never heard what happened with him and the Asian, or his kid, but part of me hopes he is miserable.

Luckily the brothers don't care about filling my room so for the rest of the semester I get to have a private room. I even pull off the best grades of my college career with a 3.6 GPA.

Chapter 7

I am alone. By choice for once. Instead of going home for Christmas I decide to stay at the frat house. When finals end, there is the typical huge party followed by a day of recovering from the night before. Then everyone took off. I don't care to go home this year. My mother and father decided they were going to take a cruise, leaving me with the choice of being in Utah or California for Christmas. Either way I am alone but at least in California I don't have to freeze.

Before Arnold left he invited me to Nor Cal to spend Christmas with him and his family, but I told him I wanted some time alone. Truly I just don't see the point in crashing some other family's Christmas. Not only am I awkwardly staying in a stranger's house, but will suffer the even more awkward day of watching Arnold and his family on Christmas. Sitting quietly on the couch watching as children open presents from the parents and just sipping a drink to keep you occupied during that time. I could just see me desperately hoping they had a dog so I had someone to hang out with. On top of that I wouldn't have a present for anyone so it be more of a spectator in this group activity. No, it is way better to be alone on Christmas than with strangers.

Troy is the last one to leave the frat house, mainly because he was the most trashed from partying. Jocks are all the same. They party like crazy but when they know they don't have to get up for practice they go even farther by trying to keep that perfect drunken state without throwing up for the entire night.

Ever since that last night of rush week Troy has kept a safe distance from me. Like if he gets too close to me he will spontaneously combust. I guess in a sense that is true. He enters the draft next year so if I was to tell people he broke my leg he might not get drafted. Then again if I say that, I'd probably get kicked out of the frat and so would Arnold and maybe everyone because the school would be forced to close the frat. Whatever, I don't really care. My leg doesn't even hurt anymore. I wish he wouldn't treat me like I have the plague though.

"Headed home Troy?" I ask as I see him walking to the door with a bag. He gives me a little nod but doesn't look at me fully, more just allowing himself to see me in his peripherals. "Where you going for Christmas?" I ask, as he is about to touch the knob of the door.

"Arizona," he says, knowing he can't just give me another nod. He is pausing at the door as if he was stuck in time. He lets out a deep breath and turns to me. "You want to come with?"

I know he is offering because of guilt and I have no intention of going, but I can't let this opportunity pass. "Where in Arizona?" I respond.

His face grows a little pale as he realizes that I am considering his feeble offer. "Ah...Prescott," he says, rubbing his head as if trying to wipe sweat that hasn't fallen yet.

I smile and pretend to think for a moment. With each passing second I can see him becoming more and more worried that I may say yes. "Do you have to leave like right now?" I know I don't want to go but I can't help tug the chain just a little longer. It's taking all the strength I have not to start busting up laughing.

"Yeah, I got to go before traffic gets bad," he responds nervously.

"Well, I would need to do a little packing first." In an instant his eyes fill with fear as if a bus was about to hit him. I look down at his hand holding the bag and see the tight fist he is making. If that bag string were a person's neck, the head would have popped off by now. My words bring him fear and I can't help but smile. He probably thinks that my happiness is to have somewhere to go but watching this giant squirm is so much more fun. I turn and make my way to the stairs. "Actually, I will rain check that. Maybe next time I'll go with you but I just remembered, I got plans with this girl I met at the party." Of course I'm lying.

"Alright, later," he says with relief as he darts out of the house. I think he wants to get out of there before I change my mind.

That three minute interaction will make me smile for at least a week – the thought that I made a football player shake in his shoes like a little baby.

The first three days alone in the frat house are relaxing. I mostly just watch TV and drink whatever liquor was left around. I'm not saying that I was drunk for the first three days but I definitely keep a good buzz on for 12 hours a day.

After I get tired of drinking I decide to do a little exploring. I go to the school to see what it is like when no one is there. What I find is amazing. Nothing. I find nothing. Everything is quiet and there is nothing to do. All the buildings are locked up except for the library, but why would I want to go in there? It isn't too long after that I am greeted by campus security.

"What are you doing here?" an out of shape security guard yells at me as he struggles out of his campus-issued golf cart. He has one hand on his pepper spray and the other hand resting on that big gut of his.

"Just walking around," I say, then turning to continue on my path.

"You can't be here," he tells me.

"Why."

"The campus is closed. I will have to escort you off," he says in what I expect he thinks is his intimidating voice. How dangerous it must be to be a campus security guard when the school is closed. Wonder if his mother is okay with the dangerous lifestyle he leads.

"Fine." I make my way over to him and he jerks out his pepper spray and points it at me and fires it at me. Jumping back I barely escape the stream followed by making a few incoherent words. "What are you doing?"

"Y-you stay back," he says with a little stutter in his voice. I can see he is just as frightened as me, except I don't have freaking pepper spray in my hand.

"What the hell moron! I was just getting in the cart!" I scream at him, trying to figure out if I am in the line of the possible second attack of the pepper stream.

"It's against school policy to let students ride in the security vehicles," he responds, slowly lowering the pepper spray just a bit, but still at the ready in case I "attack him" again.

"No it's not, I have see girls get plenty of rides."

"That's a safety concern," he says, but I know that's bull. I see girls riding the cart, and the security guards uses the free shuttle service to fail miserably at hitting on girls who are way, way out of their league.

I make my way back to the frat house with Officer Fatty behind me. I can hear his foot slip off the gas every so often, after the sixth time I am really tempted to turn around and slap him, but he still has that pepper spray in his hand. After twenty minutes of being stalked by campus police, I finally get back to the house. I walk up the stairs and turn around.

"Thanks for the escort," I say sarcastically.

"Hey you show me respect!" he demands.

"You show me a push up and I'll show you some respect." I go into the house but I can hear him get out of his golf cart for a second and then sit down quickly. He takes off at a blazing 5mph but I know he can still hear my mocking laughs.

A week alone in the frat house turns into a big mistake. I become restless and find myself getting drunk at 3:00pm just so I could be hungover the next day so I have something to do, even if that thing is hugging the toilet.

Christmas Day is an especially good day. Instead of opening presents I open my brothers' rooms. Their secrets are my presents.

The first room I go in was Chris's, the head of the frat. He is one of few in the frat who have their own room. I find the typical crap – dirty magazines, condoms, and some private liquor. The one interesting thing I do find was some pills kept in an unmarked bottle hiding in his sock drawer. Seeing the number on the pill I was sadly disappointed by what it was. Methylphenidate, an A.D.D. drug. I've heard people talk about this stuff. Ten to one says that he doesn't have any kind of attention deficit but probably uses them when he has a test. It's kind of a smart thing to do. I have heard of people doing it to get a boost before a test. I grab three pills, enough that he wouldn't notice, and I leave his room, making sure not to leave any clues I was in there.

The second room I go to is Chad's, that tool that tricked me and the other pledges into cleaning up after the party that he was supposed to clean up. The room was trashed and has a foul odor of rotting fruit. I don't worry about covering my tracks. It's not like he would notice, heck, with the state it's in, anything I move would be an improvement. If I were Chad's roommate I would tell him to stop being a slob. I don't know who Chad's roommate is though. The room is very boring but I do make one terrifying discovery. Under his bed in a suitcase is an entire female outfit. I don't know if it belongs to him or a girl he had over, but after finding that, I get out of there before I discover something worse.

I make my way down the halls, just opening and closing doors. If there isn't something catching my eye I don't go in. When I get to Troy's room I turn the knob and walk forward. The door is locked and I end up jamming my shoulder against the door. I jiggle the handle for a bit, hoping that the movement will somehow convince the door to open, but to no avail. Staring at the door I wonder what Troy keeps in his room. He lives on the third floor so going in through the window is not an option.

I stop going through rooms and imagine what is in that locked room. Part of me hopes that there are steroids or something that would get Troy in trouble. If only I could figure out a way to get in there.

The next day I make my way back into one of the brothers' rooms, I think his name is Brian, or Ryan. I am not really sure. People don't really enunciate his name well enough for me to know either way. All I know is he makes some extra cash on the side dealing pot. People knew he did drugs, but when Colorado legalized pot they all thought he brought it from back home. I remember, well partially remember, 'cause we were talking during a party, but he said something like weed in Colorado was too expensive. That makes me think his supplier is someone not in that state. Either way I go to his room and find his stash of joints he keeps in his secret hiding place, the air vent. He has like over a hundred pre-rolled joints, so I figure he wouldn't miss one.

I had never smoked pot before and figure while I'm alone here it'd be the best time. Heck if I freak out, at least I'd do it alone so people don't mock me. It takes me a while to get the nerve to smoke though, so I have a couple shots of whiskey first. Well, it wasn't so much shots but swigs from the bottle.

I light the joint and take a few puffs. The first couple puffs cause me to cough and gag. My stomach begins to hurt and I feel as if I will throw up at any moment. Suddenly the nausea goes away and I start to feel as if everything is getting better. The next thing I remember is waking up naked on the couch cuddling with a box of cereal. I have candy wrappers and other empty boxes of food around me as well, and a slight headache. I find finished joints but also a couple more unsmoked ones. I go up to Brian's, or Ryan's room to see the air vent cover open and a bunch of joints dumped out in front of it. I must have come up for more and thrown them all on the ground. I put them all back in the bag, close the vent, and get out of that room. I think about borrowing a few more joints from Brian or Ryan but decide it would be a bad idea. I might just smoke 'em all.

It's a good thing I didn't smoke anymore than I did 'cause Brian or Ryan came back the next day. He never said anything about missing a couple of joints so I figure he never noticed. It's funny. I get yelled at for using all the air freshener that I used to cover up the weed smell, but not for smoking or drinking half of the frat's liquor. If only they knew what I did here while they were all gone.

Chapter 8

I have been to hell. It is Calculus. This class is, by far, the most soul-crushing class that has ever been. The teacher shows up late for every class and makes sure everyone knows that he doesn't want to be there. He doesn't like to answer questions and seems personally offended when someone doesn't understand the material right away. Luckily, I am good at math so I never have to question what he is teaching. I feel sorry for one girl in the class. She once asked a question and he said that he didn't have time to help someone who learns so slow and told her to go to the math lab. I don't blame people who have trouble in this guy's class. He has probably the heaviest Indian accent and his writing is crap. Makes you wonder why schools hire people who are so unintelligible in speaking and writing.

Hello! We're in America! We don't speak broken English!

The only good thing about being in Calc is that Emily is in class right next door, so we get out about the same time and we head over to the cafeteria and get lunch every Monday and Wednesday. I have noticed lately that Emily always has her hair curled these days. She used to just keep it down or in a ponytail, but now it's always done like she's about to get pictures taken. I never say anything because it just seems like an odd thing to talk to a girl about.

We start our conversation the same way every time. How's classes going, you passing everything, yada yada yada. After that we get to the interesting part of the conversation. I don't understand why we just don't start with the interesting stuff but I guess it's just habit.

In the middle of taking a bite from her salad she gives me a quick look. "So I went out with that guy," she says right before shoving a big bite in her mouth.

"Which guy?" I ask, because there could be a dozen guys she could be talking about. I just hope her answer isn't Troy.

"Remember that guy I told you about who asked me out like three times and I kept blowing him off?" she says with her mouth stuffed, covering her mouth so I don't see the food in her mouth.

"Yeah, well, I remember you telling me about him. I don't know his name though."

"Well, his name is Max, and he asked me out again." She says this with a smile so I already know she said yes but just to give the benefit of the doubt I respond.

"And?"

"I said yes, but, you know, nonchalantly, you know, so it didn't sound like I was desperate." She talks about him taking her to a museum and then dinner and ended with kissing her at the door of her dorm room. She goes into great detail about every little thing, from the paintings they stopped and looked at to what the waitress was wearing. Most of the details are boring but seem to be very important to her. "We are going out again next week," she says, finishing her story.

"Next week? That seems odd. Why such a large gap between dates?" I ask.

"Well, he's got family stuff to go to this weekend and he said it would just be easier to do it when he gets back."

Again this seem too perplexing to me. "Why don't you two just go out during the week then?"

She gives me a look that I had only seen one other time. When Troy hit on her and she had to pretend like she was interested in her for my sake. "Because he cares about his and my grades too much to risk it with a late night date. I mean, we text a lot, but being in the same room would be too distracting."

I say nothing else about her and Max, afraid that somehow I would offend her with basic reason. We leave on good terms, even though for a moment it seemed like she was one breath away from cussing me out and leaving in a fury.

The semester seems to blow by. There is nothing interesting to keep me busy, but enough happens that makes time not stand still. Still, but nothing to brag about to my friends back home. Doesn't keep me from making crap up but I wish that half the stories I told them were real.

I don't see much of Emily at the end of the semester. If she isn't in class she is with Max. We text here and there but don't get lunch as often as we use too. I understand that she'd rather hang out with her boyfriend than me. Heck, if I had a girlfriend, I'd rather make out with her than talk to Emily.

Finals end and I go home, that long trip through Vegas and back to Utah. I can't wait until I am 21 and can stop here and spend a night or two gambling and partying before going back home.

I am especially excited for my junior year. Not because I hit the halfway point but because I will finally get to register somewhat early. The first two years I was at the bottom of the barrel. Getting the last sign-up date automatically gives you the earliest and latest classes, but this time it's all 1 p.m. to 4 p.m. classes for me. Heck, I might just schedule all my classes for Monday and Wednesday so I can have five days off.

When I look up my grades, I see that I got Bs in every class but one. Calculus. The class that I aced two tests and B'd the third, I end up with a D+ in the class. Blindsided I see my perfect schedule disappear. My body shakes. I didn't know how that could have happened. Even if I failed the final I should have wound up with a C+ in the class. The final was only 15% of our total grade. I quickly email the teacher, hoping that I can get him to change my grade before class registration starts next week.

Dear Prof. Pillai:

I looked up my grades and saw that I got a D+ in your calculus class on M/W. I was wondering what I got on the final and if there was anything I could do to get my grade up to a C so that I can continue down my education path. If I don't pass this class I will have to repeat this year with just this one class.

Thank you

Tyler Freed

I don't hear from him for three days. Each day is more and more terrifying. Just the idea of repeating a semester drives me crazy. It had to have been a mistake because I was one of the smarter students in that class.

On the fourth day after I sent him that email I got a response.

Tyler

You got a 72% on the test. Your homework brought your grade down.

That was all he wrote and I knew there had to be some kind of mistake. I knew homework was a big percentage of our grades but knew I turned in almost all of it. So I emailed him again.

Dear Prof. Pillai:

Thank you for responding so quickly. I am wondering what was the problem with my homework grade. I know I did almost all of it. Can you please clarify that for me?

Thank you

Tyler Freed

Another four days go by. Even though I thank him for responding quickly he was anything but fast.

By the time he does respond, he tells me that I got only 38 of 225 possible homework points. I know this was wrong and he told me after another couple of days that if I wanted to prove it I would have to drop the homework outside his box that Friday. He would change my grade if I were right.

That Thursday I make my way back to the campus spending another $150 on gas. I get to the frat house and find all my old assignments. Luckily I was told to always hold onto my homework, just in case the teacher never put them into his grade book. I count up the homework and discover I have 199 of the 225 points. Knowing that they were enough for a C at least in the class, I make my way to his office early Friday morning, but something tells me to give him only copies. Instead of going to his office, I go to the library and scan all the homework and then email him the PDFs. In my email, I ask him to email me when he changes my grade so I can be ready to apply for classes next semester.

I do not hear from him all weekend so I email him again that next Monday, and when I don't hear from him Tuesday, I write him again and again until the following Monday when he finally responds.

Tyler,

I have received your email but I had made an error in my calculations. With your homework you get a C- and will still need to retake the class.

After maybe a fifteen or twenty minute rant, I email the chair of the math department about what happened and ask for her help in solving the problem. For a week I do not get an email back. When I email her a second time, she responds the next day. She says that she will be willing to help but said my email was very confusing and asked me to email her again and try to be clearer. I don't know how I could be clearer? Teacher lost my homework and now is making up bullshit to keep me away from the grade I deserve. Would that make it clearer? I write that, but then quickly delete it and write a more formal email.

Again she waits a week to respond to me. It's not like my response is a surprise to her. I explained the desperate situation I am in. Like, come on, I had already missed my original registration date and now I will be lucky if I can get all the classes I need

Dear Mr. Freed:
I have talked to Prof. Pillai about your grade and he assures me that it is correct. I agree with him and wish you luck in your upcoming semester.
Ms. Morgan.

This seems to me like it should have been an easy win, yet somehow I lose. There has to be a mistake so I called the Dean's office and made an appointment, telling them that I have an issue with a teacher's grading.

I sit outside the Dean's office for nearly an hour. My appointment is for 1:00 p.m. but I don't get in until 1:45 p.m. The Dean greets me and apologizes for the wait and invites me to sit down. Finally, I think, I will get some help.

"Here's the thing. I was given a final grade of a D+ and when I emailed the teacher he said I was missing a lot of homework. When I proved he made a mistake, he told me he made an error in his grading and that I was still going to need to repeat the class." The Dean nods along and follows my story completely, which makes me happy because I'm sure she'll say I'm right.

"I am sorry but I can't help," she said.

"Why not?" I asked.

She plays with some papers for a bit. "We have a chain of command and when it comes to student issues with grades you have to go to the teacher and then the Chair of that department."

"I did!" I quickly interrupt. "I emailed the Chair, Ms. Morgan, and she said she agreed with Pillai, and I know they both made a mistake."

"Really," she pauses for a moment. "Well, again, I am sorry, but I can't help you. What I can do is point you to the Grade Dispute Committee.

"What's that?" I ask, confused.

"It's a committee that will hear your case and then make a decision based on both your and Professor Pillai's stories."

"Okay, cool, so when can I talk to this committee?"

"You actually missed the cut-off so you will have to wait until November 14th."

"Missed the cut-off? When was the cut-off?" I demanded to know.

"Last week."

"What! Come on! I can't wait a semester to get my grade! I need it now!" The volume of my voice is now becoming very difficult to control as my emotions spin out of control.

"I'm sorry but even if they hear your complaint they wouldn't be able to give you a verdict until end of the year."

"So it would be a year until I could get my grade?"

"Yes," she says with a smile. Why the heck is she smiling right now? This is not happy news. This is push back my graduation back a year and cost me more money. They are pretty much screwing me out of more tuition. Thieves! That's what they are.

"Screw it, I'll just take the class next semester," I say storming out of her office and slamming the door as I leave.

"You okay?" asks the secretary.

"No, the freaking math teacher lost my homework and the chair took too long to get back to me and now I have to take the class over." Far too much information I told this girl but it all just came out.

"Pillai?" she asked.

"Yeah, how did you know?" I ask.

"He and Sandra are dating."

"Sandra?"

"Sandra Morgan, the Chair of the Math Department," she responds before going back and typing something on her computer.

What the Hell! The Chair and Pillai are screwing each other? No wonder she took so long to reply, she was freaking stonewalling me to protect him.

"Hey, how do I complain about a teacher?" I ask the secretary.

"I wouldn't bother. He's got tenure so he is pretty much protected. You could complain but it does nothing. Yeah, you're pretty much just screwed."

It's sad but this secretary is the most helpful out of anyone. At least she tells me the truth. Teachers here are a protected class. As long as they aren't sleeping with a student they can't get in trouble.

I go back to the frat house. I sneak into Brian's or Ryan's room and grab another joint. I throw it on my bed and head down to the first floor looking for any liquor I can find. Sadly the only thing I can find is the cheap vodka that tastes like sweat. Doesn't matter what it taste like, it serves its purpose and gets me good and drunk. I lock my door and move the desk in front of the door. Lighting up the joint, I slowly feel all the pain that the school inflicted on me dissipate.

A wasted semester. That's what next year will be, one class that I should have passed and a bunch of pointless classes. I need at least 12 units to live in the frat and since it's a school requirement, I doubt I can get around this one. At least I will have enough time to get wasted.

Chapter 9

Rush Week. A time that put me through an extreme amount of mental and physical pain. Part of me is excited to watch as incoming pledges bow down to me, and watch as they are forced to find me a girl, or understand the excruciating feeling of their insides burning from hot food and stupid challenges.

The pledges come to the first night of Rush Week and the new head of the house, Mitch, greets them the same way that Chris greeted us a year ago. Instead of sending the pledges off on the challenge right away, he tells them to introduce themselves to the brothers.

I lean on the wall with Arnold as we watch the new blood near to pissing themselves as they introduce themselves to the brothers.

"Do you think we were like that one?" says Arnold, using his drink filled hand to point at a pledge who looks like he had dunked his head under a faucet.

"Nah," I say taking a drink out of my glass. "No one was that nervous that they sweat that much."

"What do you think Mitch is going to have them do? Get him a burrito, or find us dates, or maybe keep it simple and do a beer pong tournament."

"I don't know Arnold. I know what I would do if I was in charge." I chuckle and glance over at Arnold, who is curious. Truthfully, I don't have a single idea, but if given the opportunity to plan Rush Week, I could probably figure out a couple dozen random challenges that would make the pledges cry and quit.

A new pledge gives Arnold and me a nod from across the room and walks over. Already I hope that this guy doesn't get in. He just reeks of tool, everything from his neon tank top to his multicolored shoes. A part of me wants to grab a balloon just so I could pop it on his over-the-top spiked hair. I wonder if I threw an orange at his hair, would the spikes skewer the fruit?

"Yo bro, I'm TJ," the pledge says not waiting for us to reach out and shake his hand. Instead he grabs our hands in the half secret handshake that just feels like a squid in my grasp.

"Good to meet you," I say, hoping that he would go on to the next brother, but he doesn't. He proceeds to lean against the wall with Arnold and me. I might have been fine with it but he starts to tell us his life story. I don't know if I forgot to take off my "please tell me your life story like we are close" shirt, but he goes on for along time. Maybe it's five minutes but it seems like an hour to me. Arnold asks questions and throws in the occasional "cool story," but I'm not sure if he's serious or just messing with him. That's the trouble with Arnold – he doesn't seem to ever have a problem with anyone, at least he never acts like he does. Sometimes I wonder if he actually considers us friends or just is too nice to say anything.

"Dude, we totally have to hit the gym sometime," TJ says to Arnold.

"I'm not a gym person," responds Arnold.

"Dude, come on. A little bench press and a few grunts and you will have the ladies all over you." He uses the word "dude" way too often. It must be a verbal tic or something. I can see he is trying to get in good with the brothers, anyone who knows Arnold knows him and exercise don't mix. He will spend the rest of his life fat. He knows it and everyone else knows it.

"Alright listen up!" Mitch calls out. Finally the moment I have been waiting for, watching as stupid challenges torture the new pledges. "I want to thank all of you for coming. I hope that you all had a chance to meet as many brothers as you could. We will call you in the upcoming days to let you know if you are in the frat. If you don't get a call, better luck next year."

My jaw nearly breaks off its hinges as I push through a group of exiting pledges to make my way to Mitch. "What the hell? Aren't we doing any challenges or anything? I wanted to pepper spray some sorry-ass pledge in the face."

Mitch looks at me like I'm completely mad. He folds his arms and looks down at me with a expression a parent may have towards their child when they are stunned to see their baby biting the TV. "I'm a little shocked to hear you of all people say that."

"What do you mean?" I ask.

He places his right hand on my shoulder and gives it a light squeeze. The squeeze of my shoulder making me drop my shoulder to escape his touch. For a second I consider pushing his arm off but withhold my annoyance. "After what happened last year I thought it would be best to be more mellow in the way we accept new pledges."

"That's not fair! I got pepper sprayed, feet cut, choked down hot peppers, and got my leg broken! And that was only one day! I waited a year to do the same thing!"

"You want to break someone's leg?" asks Mitch in a Mr. Rogers-type voice.

"No, I just want it to be fair."

"Well, that's not your decision. It's mine." With that, he takes his hand off my shoulder and walks away.

I tell Arnold what Mitch told me and he seems okay with the decision to make it just a vote instead of a contest filled with strenuous challenges. Later that night Mitch asks us to vote in favor of at least six of the pledges. I had only met the one, TJ, but I refuse to even vote for him. No way I was voting for someone who just shows up for a single night. After all the shit I had to go through, those idiots should have to at least get pepper sprayed.

Mitch makes the calls Friday and tells us that the five new brothers who received the most votes will move in that Monday.

Saturday I leave my room with a note on the wall saying that one of the new brothers will move into my room. I try to convince them to move Arnold in with me but said that it was already decided. Which means, "We don't like you and are going to torture you." They have done this for a year – for some reason they all have this resentment for me. I'm surprised that they haven't gotten Arnold to hate me yet either. Who gives a crap. I'm here 'til I graduate and I don't care how much it sucks, 'cause it will suck for them that much more.

On Monday I return from class and see my new roommate. I wonder if they will ever just straight up and tell me that they hate me and want me to leave, or will they continue to do these passive aggressive moves? Lo and behold, I open my door and see TJ, flexing his guns in this skinny, tall mirror he brought from home. Upon seeing me he puts on a very cut up tank top that wouldn't count as a shirt in most restaurants.

"Dude! So awesome we're roomies!" says TJ, as he quickly bounces like a puppy over to me and gives me a sweaty hug. I push him off but he just keeps smiling. "Dude, I hope you don't mind but I ran out of room in my closet so I stored some vodka under your bed." He gives me a wink and then goes back to staring at himself in the mirror.

"No problem," I tell him. Throwing my bag onto my bed, I leave while he is distracted by his own image. Another year with a crap roommate. Hey, if he brings backs a girl constantly I'll just give him the old hole-in-the-condom treatment.

This semester has been a bird. I have been flying through all of my classes with zero issues on grades. Freaking calculus is the only real class I am taking. The others are an American History class, which is pretty much the stuff you learn in middle school. I do like that class. The teacher offers 15% extra credit so if I just write a ten page paper on one of the presidents, I don't have to do the final. The third class is an English class Arnold convinced me to take. We are assigned to read a few old stories and then we are tested on them the next class. Probably the easiest class to cheat on because the teacher spends the test time texting her new boyfriend. The fact that she talks about her love life to the class just makes her seem sad and desperate to have other people know that someone wants her. The final class is this piano class. It's an easy class that I show up to once a week so I can learn how to do simple note stuff and then at the end of the year I have to play like a two sheet song in front of the class. I have to also go see five concerts and do write-ups for them. Literally being forced to go see concerts. If only every class was so difficult.

Emily and I have grown farther and farther apart in the last few months. At first I thought it was because she was technically a year ahead of me now and just busy with her upper division classes, but even then I expect to get a text every so often. I send her a message online but don't hear anything back for two days. I resend the message, just in case the first one didn't actually get sent. When she does reply, I am met with a very long and overwhelming message.

"Hi Tyler. I don't really know how to start this but I wanted to thank you for your friendship all these years. I truly believe that without each other, college would have been a much more difficult process for both of us. I will always remember fondly the random drives we took to get 2 am burritos. There comes a time that two people reach an impasse and there is nowhere else to go and they have to just say goodbye. As you know I have been dating Max for six months now and things are getting serious. I don't think it would be wise for me to spend so much time with other guys because I think that it would make Max feel jealous, and I do not want to put him through that, so I think it would be best if we don't hang out or talk anymore. Thank you for your friendship and I wish you luck in the rest of college and life."

I reread the message at least five times trying to make sure that I am reading it correctly. After all those reads, I come to the same conclusion I had when I read it the first time. She sent me a freaking break-up letter! After two years of friendship she is kicking me to the curb. For what? A guy she's dating! Not even a guy who is her fiancé but just a freaking boyfriend! Tomorrow she could find him in bed with another girl and she is telling me, her best friend in college, that we can't be friends anymore.

Feeling betrayed, I get up and go to my bed. I reach underneath and pull out one of the bottles of vodka that TJ stores under there. A moment of happiness comes over me as I taste the good stuff. Over and over I reread Emily's message.

She wants to thank me for our friendship? If you want to thank me for being your friend then keep freaking being my friend! Is it really that hard to continue being friends with someone? I wonder if she broke up with all her friends or if it was just me? For each sentence I took a swig of vodka. And I continue to obsess over the message. Max feels jealous, of what, a platonic friendship? We never dated! I never even freaking asked you out. I mean like when I first met her I thought she was cute and wouldn't mind dating her but I never asked her out so that is moot. She can't freaking do that crap. I messaged her back.

"Emily, what the hell are you talking about? If Max is jealous of me then maybe you should tell him that he doesn't have to worry or maybe get us to meet and let him to see for himself that I'm not a threat. Also if he has this much power over you maybe you shouldn't be dating this guy. If he makes you not have guy friends when you are dating imagine how life will be if you married this guy. You'll be one of those shut-in wives who has to ask her husband's permission to do anything."

I figured she would respond in a few days or not at all but about three minutes later I got a response.

"Tyler! I can't believe how rude you are being. You are totally being disrespectful and trying to ruin my relationship with Max. Instead of being an asshole you could be a little more supportive."

"Emily, You are telling me we can't be friends anymore! You are being the disrespectful asshole. I hope you get what you deserve."

She never responds to me after that. I would never see or talk to that girl again. I sit at my desk shaking the bottle of vodka as the pain in my heart slowly grows smaller with the volume of the bottle.

Suddenly TJ opens the door to see me drunk off his vodka. His tool tan face becomes red with rage as he holds his hands up but couldn't find what words to say. I give him a wave with his vodka bottle and take another swig.

"Dude, what the hell do you think you're doing!" says TJ, as he rushes over and grabs the half empty bottle of vodka from me.

I try to focus on him and yell back, but I can't keep him in the center of my vision. "I-I," I mutter. "Emily broke up with me," I tell him.

"Dude, what? That totally sucks dude," he says. "Didn't even know you had a girlfriend."

Realizing he misunderstood me I am about to correct him, but then he grabs a cup from on top of our mini refrigerator and pours me a glass. TJ asks me how we met and how long we knew each other. I answer all his questions, but never let on that we never dated. Part of me wants to punch him for using the word "dude" in every sentence, but for free vodka I can take it. By the end of the bottle he must have been at least buzzed but I am nearing blackout. The last thing I remember is hitting my head when I fall down trying to get out of the chair.

I wake up in the middle of the night on the floor cuddling with a trash can. My blanket is covering my head but it can't protect me from the hangover that is coming over me. Slowly getting up, I see TJ sleeping in my bed. If the pain in my head wasn't so bad I would pull him straight off, but I don't plan on sleeping anymore. Instead I grab some painkillers from my desk, ones that I stole from one of the brothers, and walk out of the frat house.

Still a little woozy and half asleep, I walk in the cool night air. I find myself in the middle of the campus and sit on a bench and watch the sun take the place of the moon. Students walk past as I continue to stare at a building in front of me. Sitting there until the sun begins to set, I walk back to the frat house. I know I've missed my classes for the day but I don't care. Another crap semester down the drain.

Chapter 10

The Pyramids – the greatest accomplishment the Egyptians ever achieved. When people go to Egypt they want to see the freaking pyramids because they are awesome. You know what is awesome? My pyramid of beer cans. One semester of hard labor created this amazing structure of architectural drinking, a combination of light, domestic, and foreign beer cans. I find it mesmerizing – this wonder of the AKA house. Over 100 beer cans in perfect balance. Putting them up there was no easy task but when you don't take many classes, drinking becomes more than a hobby you do Thursday through Sunday. It becomes a weeklong marathon. The best thing about this marathon is that I didn't have to practice or pace myself. I just did it!

I go to my American history final and I think I answer a question about the Civil War with BEARS! Wish I could see the look on the teachers face when he grades my test and there's BEARS! Doubt that tool will even grade the test. I bet he's got some teaching assistant he pays to grade them. Probably some cute undergrad he wants, but wants to make sure she won't tell the school about it. Heck, I wish I had the stones to write in the middle of one paper "fail me if you read this, moron." That would be a good test for the teacher. Those morons don't even read the papers I bet, even with a teaching assistant. Who would? Those things are like ten pages long and they get at least 30 per class, and they have to get them back to you in a week. Bullshit! They read the first paragraph and the last paragraph. If you nail those two you can just add filler through the rest of the paper.

I don't even go to my piano final. Lost 15% on my final grade but I had a 97% going in, no point in going to the final. Bs get degrees. English was probably the easiest class of the semester. I got teamed up with this girl for "peer review," which is pretty much the teacher saying I don't want to do the added work of grading and I want "me time" during class, so for the first 30 minutes of class read each other's crap and tear it apart. Then there is Calculus. I swear I got the one freaking American in the entire math department and this guy was a total idiot. I'm not saying he shouldn't teach, because he made class incredibly easy, but he needs to practice in front of a mirror or something. The guy just couldn't make a career doing public speaking. You'd think after a semester he would be more comfortable in class. Hell, at least he kept all my homework. Walked out of the class with B- and didn't even study. That's what you got to do – find a class you can easily pass and take it. Just get that piece of paper that proves you finished college.

As soon as I take that last final, I get in the car and drive back home for winter break. Never thought I'd be excited for a twelve hour drive. Stop in Vegas. I'm not 21 yet but I figure I'll throw five in a slot machine and try my luck. The lights, the sounds, not as exciting as I thought it would be. Guess I have to come back here when I'm 21 and get trashed to play. After just two spins of the wheel on a penny slot I lose my five bucks. Not wanting to get caught, I take my leave and make my way back to Utah.

Being home is like spending time in a stranger's house. My parents, well, mom at least, is happy to see me, but after a little time they act as if they don't understand why I am still there. I just stay out of their way and try to spend time with people from high school. That isn't fun but it's something to do. I have to fill the hours of the day somehow. I go to the movies and go to the mall, but after two or three hours I'm ready to go home.

It's the same crap over and over. "How is college? My college is amazing, I'm having the best time of my life. Remember that one time senior year?" Like I said, it fills the hours and I do enjoy getting out of the house.

I come home from getting coffee with a guy from high school and my parents are sitting in the living room. They call me over and ask me to sit down. Whenever parents ask you to sit down you know something shitty is about to happen. You automatically expect the worst. My mind is like a computer as I think of a million things that they could tell me. Are they getting a divorce? Did someone die? Did the company go under? Did I get kicked out of school? What?

"Tyler," my mom starts, taking a deep breath before she continues. I know it's something emotional – if it wasn't my father would be telling me. "After some time thinking about this, your father and I have decided that it would be best," she pauses again as I move to the edge of the couch. I start to wonder what is so bad but the only thing I can think of is that they won't help pay off my student loan. If that is the case, I'm screwed. She takes another deep breath and speaks softly, "We are going to accept an offer on the company."

I sit there silent. Not knowing what to say I just look at my father and his stern expression and then back at my mom who, as usual, seems overly emotional. Finally after a few moments of awkward silence waiting for them to say something I ask, "What does that mean?"

"It means we," she says pointing to my father and back to her, "are retiring." She pauses again. Her pausing is driving me insane. I keep expecting her to say something like, "and we are moving to Alaska so get out." "I'm sorry, I know you were expecting to have a job waiting for you when you graduate but, well, you will have to find something else."

She stops again as I see a tear run down her face. I wish that she would transfer some of her overflowing emotional dysfunction to my father.

One, then I could see some kind of emotion out of my father, and two, I wouldn't have to hear her whining all the time over and over about the most pointless things. She must save it all for me, 'cause if she did this in front of her clients, they would just find another agent.

I want to get up and go to my room but I know if I leave now I will get nothing out of the sale. "So," I pause to mirror my mom's reaction just slightly. "Are you happy?"

"Yeah," my father says quickly.

"Well, it was a good offer and your father and I want to do some traveling before we get too old."

"Okay," I say, slowly getting up and making my way towards my room. Out of the corner of my eye I see my mom's hand raise slightly as if she wants me to stop and then she drops her hand to her side as quickly as she raised it. I can see in my mom's face, the guilt inside her. She forced me into my major, and now there is no job for me when I finish. It's amazing! Now I can get whatever I want and she will try to make up for what she thinks I lost. She is tied around my finger and she doesn't even know it. My father doesn't even realize that she is going to force him to do something to make me feel better. I don't know how I will use this power but it will come to me soon.

I knew that when I finished school things might be difficult. My plan was that I would search for a job right before graduation and if I couldn't find something for $60,000, I could fall back on my parents for work. They'd probably give me like $15 an hour but I'd be doing things a high school dropout should be doing – putting flyers in mailboxes and just following my parents around waiting for them to tell me what to do. Now I get half my tuition paid for and I'm not forced to degrade myself to slave status. No slavery no guilt.

"Tyler." Mom knocks and opens the door.

"What's up," I say in a monotone voice.

"I was talking to your father, and we feel awful about leaving you high and dry." Meaning she feels guilty and my father doesn't want to fight with her. "We will use some of the money we get from the business and pay for a little more of your college."

Now I am so excited that I can't pretend to be sad anymore. "How much?" I blurt out.

Pausing at my sudden change of mood she stares at me for a moment. I quickly change my expression to a calmer yet still happy look.

"$40,000," she says.

$60,000 is all I will have to pay for college. That's nearly just one semester of school I have to pay for. Here I thought it would take me ten years to pay off my student loans with them paying half, but with another 40 grand I can pay it off in like five years when I get a job. Those idiots who took out loans will spend years in debt and I will be living the high life. I love it.

I thank my mom and when I see my father I thank him for the added help, but I make sure I sound sad for the end of the family company just to make sure they don't take away my $40,000.

The day after Christmas, I head back to college. New Year's was especially fun, I just wish I could remember her name. After 11 beers I seem to have trouble with names. I remember everything that happens but I struggle with names. It's just nice having the other guy have to sleep on the couch for a change. She gets out of bed and quickly grabs her stuff and leaves without a word to make that shameful trip from wherever she came from. I watch as she sneaks out of bed and leaves but don't make a noise to let her know I'm aware of her sluttiness. If she only turned around for a second she would see me watching her but I think she is already loathing last night's mistake. Hey, I don't mind being the mistake.

After a semester of wasted pointlessness, I am finally in the upper division of my college life. I don't know why they even bother with that lower division stuff. I honestly can't remember one bit of biology or physics. Seriously, it's been a year or two and I would get every question on a test wrong, and they think that it will prepare me for the future? Idiots. College should really just be two years of intense training in the specific field of your major. But hey, it's a great strategy to get another 100k out of students' pockets.

TJ and Arnold's roommate Alex come to my room a few days before the start of the new semester. As usual TJ uses the word "dude" in every single sentence and he's covered head to toe in his douchiest outfit. After a few minutes of pointless talking he finally gets to what he's come to talk about.

"Dude, Tyler. I know we are tight and stuff dude, but I think me and Alex are better match. So dude if you don't mind, you think it would be cool if you move in with Arnold and Alex moves in here? Like, I mean, you and Arnold are like best dudes, so it would be perfect." Damn, that guy talks like a drunk even when he is sober!

"Really, I thought we were having a good time," I lie.

"Dude, it's nothing against you, I just..." he struggles to finish.

"I understand." Heck, I wouldn't mind rooming with Arnold.

"Dude awesome! Thank you dude. Hell, I will move your stuff for you dude!"

One more "dude" and I probably would have jumped out the window. TJ and Alex spend the next hour switching rooms. The only thing I carry is my laptop. Sitting in my new bed, I ready myself for Arnold to return to tell him that Alex switched rooms. Arnold opened the door not expecting me to be there.

"Dude what are you doing here," he asks.

"Don't say that. I have heard that word enough for two lifetimes."

"What word?" he asks.

"Dude."

"Oh, okay. So what are you doing in here?" he asks pointing at all my stuff.

"Your roommate decided he wants to room with mine so we switched rooms."

"Sweet. I guess I won't have to cover my head all the time now," Arnold says. "Shoot! Forgot my other bag. Be right back." Arnold leaves the room as I jump out of the bed. I look down at the bed I was laying on. Didn't put any sheets on yet, and, just gross! Flipping the mattress, I jog down the hall and quickly strip down and shower to get off the germs that must have attached themselves to me.

Why did Arnold have to say that? I dig the soap deep into my skin as my pale white skin becomes red. I get back to my room and disinfect every surface in that place. It's like a metaphor for my current life – a clean slate or some crap like that.

Chapter 11

What do you do when you have a ten page paper due in 12 hours? You stare at the wall and wait for a wormhole to appear. You think of what you would do with super powers. How if you could sing you be the greatest performer of all time. You pretty much do anything but write that paper.

Arnold is tossing and turning in his bed, probably having a bad dream. Sometimes I hit him with a pillow but on this night, a night I must stay awake, I just watch him flop and grumble to himself because right now I find it entertaining. He has nightmares a lot but he never seems to remember having them. I wonder if he is too embarrassed by what he is afraid of, probably something stupid like kittens. Watching him for a while, I find his actions just fascinating, but when he stops I am drawn back to my computer screen and the document titled "Organizational Business" on it.

I have had this assignment for a week now. Well, we were told about it in the syllabus but I'm just now writing it. It was supposed to be a simple paper, but I never could quite find time to work on it. There was either other homework, classes to go to, or some party I couldn't miss.

Over and over I keep trying to negotiate with myself, saying, if you get this done you can get six hours of sleep...five hours...four. There's this guy I know who will write any paper for you for $100 and $10 for a homework assignment. It's a pretty good deal but I never do it, and not because I am against cheating. I have learned that the influx of cheaters in the business department is the only reason why grades are high in this major. I don't want to use the guy because I don't know if he can actually get me a good grade. If he gets me a C what am I going to do, tell the teacher it wasn't me?

Three hours until class starts. The sun is just coming up and my eyes are bloodshot. If I don't turn in this paper today I'm going to lose 15% of my final grade. There is only one option left.

8:00am. Right now every student is passing their papers up to the front of the class. The teacher is picking them up and putting them in a slightly mangled bunch in a bag. That day in class is a waste, as half the class won't learn a single thing. I, on the other hand, am in a doctor's office, patiently waiting to see the doctor.

It seems that I woke up in the middle of the night with pain in my side, teeth grinding as I clutched my stomach. After a short conversation with the doctor about waking up in a lot of pain and pointing to where it hurts, he sent me to get some quick tests. Urine, blood, and an imaging test later I was told that the pain was not my appendix but just really bad indigestion. Three hours waiting and I missed two classes. Telling the doctor that my grade has a strong attendance impact, I ask for a note. He hands me a barely legible note and I leave.

Amazing how I go from walking into the doctor with horrible pain, and a couple hours later I am gulping down a large carne asada burrito with double salsa.

I get home and email the teacher, the one who assigned, the paper due, and tell her what happened and that I am so sorry but they thought my appendix was ready to explode. A quick nap later I start working on that paper once again.

With no real deadline anymore I write that thing in just an hour. Sure, most of it is crap, but you really only need one page to explain a point.

Later that night the teacher sends me an email asking to see a doctor's note. The next day I get another email from her, this one is very sympathetic as she apologizes for her wording in the last email. I just have to bring in the paper next time I see her. A co-pay to the doctor saved my grade in that class.

I get an easy job working at the school in the Student Center. First day I show up and they tell me to sit at the desk, and if anyone comes up, answer their questions. Most days I work four hours a day and maybe talk to three people. Other days if I don't feel like doing work I just let the phone ring or ask people to hold and then "forget" to get back to them. If people complain, I tell them to go through the website to register a complaint. Most people won't do that though. The school is smart because they made the complaint process so difficult that people give up halfway through. After all, who wants to spend fifteen minutes on the school's slow server to say they were on hold forever?

There are times that I did work especially hard, but that is only when the girl in front of me is especially hot. For $10 an hour I am paid to do homework and flirt with girls passing by. Not a bad job at all. I show up late a few times and they never yell at me for it. Most the time my boss is out doing God knows what and when he does notice I'm gone he doesn't say anything. We are buds, well, he thinks we are, a compliment or getting a coffee together every so often during work hours, and I can get away with anything. It's a lot like the business world I guess. The guy who keeps his head down at his desk and does his job never gets noticed, but the guy who makes noise and friends gets all the attention. You just have to make sure that they don't expect much, so when you do the bare minimum, it's an amazing accomplishment to them.

People who work at colleges usually fail at getting out in the real world, or get the college bug and never leave. That's how my boss Joel got trapped. He worked the same job I do a few years ago and when he graduated they offered him the job he currently has. He'll never leave. The job requires little work and he gets full benefits. Sure he doesn't get a great salary but based on what work he actually does he is getting paid like $75 an hour.

I can hear Joel sing a song down the hall. That's an annoying but great habit of his. He can't sing but since he does it all the time so I know when to stop watching shows online.

"Tyler I'm getting kinda hungry. You want to head out and get some food with me?" asks Joel.

I love getting lunch with Joel. The conversation is bland and always is about video games, but lunch, which he pays for, usually takes an hour and a half, and I get paid to be there. "Yeah man, let's go!" I say enthusiastically. He always gets a kick out of how pumped I am to hang out with him. I figure it's good training for the real world. If I can make Joel feel like the greatest person in the world, I will be able to do so much more than if I tried to get ahead on merit alone.

Joel always tries to get me to hang out during my off hours, but I always tell him I have homework. He believes it. He was one of those constant studiers in college, so when I tell him I have a paper he completely understands.

Thirsty Thursday comes around, the greatest day of a college career. A day filled with music, beer, and girls. By your third year you know where to spend your time. Each party is slightly different. There are places with hot girls, but you have to pay a cover, and then other places that have just average looking girls but the drinks are free. Depending on the mood, I'm either at one or the other. Sometimes I go to both.

This last year Arnold and I have become the best beer pong players in the frat house. Not so much because we are the most talented, but because we can drink everyone under the table. After one game everyone becomes a little wobbly and their aim is off. Our aim on the other hand stays pretty good for three or four games before we start feeling it.

The thing that is most annoying with beer pong is the jocks. They are way too competitive. Instead of just having fun they act as if they will die if they don't win. There have been a few times that Arnold and I have been in scuffles because some muscle head thinks we cheated. It's not our fault they suck. Jock drunks are the worst because they already want to fight when they drink, so if they have an excuse, they are going to fight. I got punched a few times, but usually we each get a punch in before we get pulled apart. Drunks don't usually have good aim either in beer pong or their punches – the worst I ever got is a hard punch in the shoulder. Didn't feel good but better than the face.

It was like a montage in my head, ten games of beer pong and ten wins. We were unstoppable, every throw landed perfectly in those red cups full of warm beer. Just like in any game, the girls flock to the winners. Even Arnold had a girl that gave him a kiss on the lips. Did she mean to land her lips on his, I don't know, but it happened. If he could think straight I bet he would have proposed to that girl right then and there. Somewhere in the eleventh game, Arnold was drinking a beer when all the sudden he couldn't keep it down. He let out a stream that crossed the table and on the other guys we were playing. The game was over.

With help from two of the frat boys, we pushed Arnold up the stairs to our room. It was very difficult as his two legs couldn't hold him up and we three dropped him a few times, laughing and pushing. We got to our room and the other two guys left when Arnold fell in as the door opened. It was like the walruses at SeaWorld. I doubt he even could feel the fall with all that alcohol, and the fat probably is an amazing cushion.

He promptly threw up. Luckily it was on one his shirts so there was a big target for all the vomit to hit. Not wanting to smell the puke all night I wrapped the shirt into a dripping ball and throw it out the window.

"Tyler...Tyler...m-my mouth has disgusting taste," he says in drunken mumbles.

"What do you want me to do?" I ask, as I stumble to him. I grab his trashcan and put it by him in case he hurls again. His breathing is hard and his skin has a slight blue tint to it, but I'm having trouble myself seeing. Falling down against the door I just sit there for a moment as the corners of my vision get drawn in.

Arnold pushes himself up a little and points to a case of beer next to me. I open up the case and pop the top for him and me and we drink one more beer. "There's dreams in ravioli," he says.

"What?" I say, laughing hysterically at him.

He moves his arm slightly and falls on his back. His slow deep breaths move his whole body. Coughing over and over between breaths.

My vision becomes dark as I can only see Arnold now. I feel my head hit the floor and can only see his head fully. His head jerks back as a gusher of puke flies out of his mouth. Now his head spasms up and down. There is something wrong. I tell my body to move but it stays still. I can feel my arm reaching for him but it hasn't left the floor. My vision goes completely dark as I watch Arnold's body go still.

Chapter 12

Five days I have sat here, my back against the door just staring at the floor. I can hear the brothers walk in the hall as they go to and return from class. Every so often I hear a knock on the door. They ask if I need anything, but I don't answer. They only ask once and then they leave.

I don't eat and the only thing I have drunk is the rest of the beer that was in the case. Class is far from my mind. I couldn't say if there was a test or a paper due. I just don't care. This room is lonely. I want it to be filled with people, but at the same time I just don't want to see anyone. People will just make me hate the world more for leaving me here without my friend, their constant stupidity and their caring for only themselves, Arnold was the only good one in this hell.

You know Arnold, I have to be honest with you. You are one of the fattest most disgusting guys I have ever known. Honestly how does someone let themselves get so fat? Did you eat in your sleep or something. How could you ever expect to get a girl? You would crush her. I'm pretty sure you could go to jail for that. I hate you Arnold. You asshole! Stupid idiot, it's your fault! Because of you I am alone. I hate you!

I get a letter from his mom inviting me to the funeral, but I couldn't go. I said that I had tests and the teachers refused to let me make them up. Truthfully I don't even know if I will be able to finish this year. His father and brother come to pick up his stuff that weekend. They cry, I didn't see it, but I hear it. I don't make eye contact with them and leave them to deal with their son's crap. When I am sure they've gone, I return to that half empty room. I feel cold and weak.

First week back to classes, the teachers pull me aside and tell me they understood, and not to worry about what I missed. It was strange, I haven't talked to these teachers at all this year but all the sudden they know who I am and what has happened in this last week. Must have been the brothers. They must have talked to my teachers. Whatever it was, I get credit for things I didn't do. Maybe if I continue to be sad and miserable I will ace the entire year.

Sitting in class I can't focus on anything the teacher says and my mind has no train of thought.

Alone in my room I open up my phone and search through the contacts. Two names I keep scrolling over. Arnold and Emily. Two people that could solve my problem and two people who can do nothing. One is dead to me and the other, I am dead to her. Not planning on calling her I still find myself going back and forth between the names. Maybe I'm just hoping that something different is going to happen the next time I land on their names.

My mom has called a few times, and even my father called once. They are pointless conversations that solve nothing, but make them feel like they are doing something of worth. If they wanted to do something of worth they should just say they would pay for my entire college education. They won't, but it's nice to imagine.

Attention from girls has increased dramatically lately. Every couple days I got one pulling on my arm asking if there is anything they can do to make me feel better. I know what I want to say but it doesn't matter what I say. My body wouldn't be able to do anything with them anyway. Nothing is working.

I finish the year, not even half aware of where I am or what I am exactly doing there. I'm last to finish my finals in every class, and when I hand the tests to the teachers they all give me the same sympathetic look. I know I don't know much of what was on the final but it doesn't really matter. When I get my grades back they are higher then I deserve. Teachers have a secret grading policy. If they like you or feel sorry for you your grade magically goes up.

Home for part of the summer, I spend my days in my room. I have stopped talking to my old friends from high school. I just don't want to see them anymore. My parents have gone on a two week cruise to the Mediterranean, so I spend my days alone watching TV and eating anything I can find in the house. Part of me wonders, now that I am alone with no one to call me, if I died would anyone know? Would anyone care? No, I don't think so. No one would be affected. My parents would care but they wouldn't know until they come home.

When my parents get home they send me to a doctor and I get some anti-depressants. I don't think I need them but it was the only way they would allow me to go back to school. They threaten to send me to some therapist and some clinic if I didn't. I don't like taking the pills, they make my head feel light, and I don't think my brain works fully when I take them. After a week on the pills I notice I do eat more but my personality is still the same. I don't want to see people and I don't really want to go back to school, it's just better than being at home.

This time when I leave my house my father gives me a hug and slips me a couple hundred bucks. It's an odd gesture from him. I stop in Vegas on my way back. After a couple hours the money is all gone. Sleeping in my car again, I wait for the motivation to finish the rest of the trip.

Back at the frat house I am greeted with mixed reactions. Some act as if nothing has happened, while others act as if everything had just happened. I treat them both the same with a weak smile and a little pointless conversation and then go straight to my room. I leave only to get food or shower or use the restroom, but when the other brothers see me they look at me as if I shouldn't be here, yet no one has the courage to ask me to leave

I miss Arnold.

Chapter 13

Rush week has ended and the pledges have been picked. Last year I was excited to see the pledges get hazed like I was and was met with disappointment. This year I did not bother to even show up. I could hear laughing and groans of failure. If I did go down I would have ruined everyone's fun. That's what I am these days. A killjoy. I can walk in to a room and suck out all the fun. Last week I came back to the frat house and a few brothers were doing a keg stand. They instantly stopped screaming and laughing when they saw me. It's best for me just to stay out of people's way.

Sitting in bed I just look up to the ceiling not knowing what I want. "You know Arnold," I say turning my head to his bed. "I have been thinking, and you really hurt me. Why did you have to die?

You should have been able to drink more and still be fine. Do you understand how hard it's been on me?" There is no answer that I can make up that I would expect him to say. Sitting up in bed I continue to focus on his bed hoping that I am just waking up from a horrible nightmare. "I want my friend back."

There is a knock at the door.

"Yeah," I call out in a depressing tone.

The door opens and Lionel, the new head of the frat, walks in and sits down on the bed. He doesn't speak right away but looks around the room for a bit. "Hey Tyler how you doing?"

"I'm okay," I say, knowing that he knows I'm not. I pray that he is here to talk to me, to help me with the shit I'm dealing with. I could really use a real friend's help. Someone who will get me out of this pit I have found myself in.

"That's good to hear," he says giving a smile. He starts to rub his hands together like he is trying to start a fire between them. "So we were thinking, Ollie wants to have a roommate and he wondered if you wouldn't mind switching with him? That way he can get a roommate and you could have your own room to yourself."

"Sure," I say.

"Great," he says slapping his legs and jumping up to his feet. He walks to the door and turns around. "Well, just move in whenever you want. If you want any help just call." Before I can answer he is already gone.

I grab my phone from my pocket and scroll through my contacts. I get to Arnold's and pause for just a moment, and then continue to go through the list. Emily. "Should I call her?" I say out loud, hoping

I somehow get an answer. I rub my finger against the corner of the phone. The need for someone to talk to is just getting stronger and nearly impossible to resist. I click on her name and hit send. The phone rings, and rings again, over and over with no answer. I take the phone away from my ear ready to hit end when...

"Hello," say someone on the other end.

"Hello," I say back realizing that the voice on the other end is not Emily. "Hi, is this Emily?" I ask already knowing the answer.

"Sorry I think you have the wrong number."

"My bad."

"No worries, bye." The girl hangs up the phone.

Emily changed her number. I wondered when she did that? Probably changed it after our last conversation online. She wanted to make sure that I never talked to her again. Selfish girl. When I'm in need she is gone. Just like Arnold is to me I am to her – dead.

I move my stuff from Arnold's and my room to my new room. Passing a few of the brothers during the process they all avert their eyes from me so as not to make eye contact. When I have finished moving I feel a slight warm feeling. The room is half the size of my old room and the closer walls seem to make me calmer and not as anxious. Desperately looking to continue the feeling I push myself in the corner of the room, between the wall and the desk. Close, but I need more. I crawl on the floor and go under the bed. I hide from the world like a child hiding from a storm. I push myself to go to class but spend the rest of my time under this bed that has become my protection from the outside world. As long as I am under this bed I feel safe.

I have trouble sleeping. I spend nights awake under the bed just pushing against my skull against the wall, hoping I will hit the right spot that will knock me out. Liquor doesn't do a thing for me anymore. No matter how drunk I get, I can't get to sleep. I make the rounds in the house talking to every brother looking for a fix for my insomnia. $50 gets me ten pills.

Late at night I look at the ten pills and wonders if I should take them all at once. Holding them in my hand I put two in my mouth and wash it down with some beer. My brain fights the pills. I can feel my body trying to let the pills do their job but my brain tries to fight it off. Body completely still, my head becomes light and I know I am nearing sleep but my brain continues to try to keep me up.

I wake six hours later. Tired but feeling slightly better I decide to skip class for the day and take two more pills. Again my brain fights the pills but loses out again. Waking another six hours I continue to take the pills until they are gone. I have slept for nearly two days. That's two days I haven't had to think about last semester.

Every week I pay $50 for sleeping pills. It's the only way that I can get through the week. When I am strapped for cash, I sell my books from the year before. Student loans paid for the $500 books but the books get me two weeks worth of pills.

Teachers in upper division classes are just as lazy as the ones in the pointless classes we are forced to take our freshman year. To minimize the amount of work that they have to do they assign us group projects. In my Business Statistics class the teacher gives us half the class time to work on our projects. He claims that because so many of the students have jobs, it's best if he gives us time in class so that we can at least have some time to work on it. It's just because he doesn't want to teach. Tenure is cheapening the quality of education I am receiving at this stupid place. If teachers depended on successful students to keep their jobs they would work a lot harder.

The class is broken up into groups of six, my group only has five though because of the class size. We got three guys and two girls. The two girls are really good friends and mostly talk to each other. The two guys are chill but besides when we meet up for the group project we don't talk. It's a good group. We get our work done and then go on with our lives. No stress, no arguments, but one of the girls, Rebecca, stares at me every once in a while. At first I thought she liked me, but catching her look at me it was not as much as a flirtatious look but more of an "I know you from somewhere" look.

One day I'm leaving the library after our group met to write our five-page update paper, when I hear someone call out for me.

"Tyler, hold up!" I turn to see Rebecca speed walking to me. Thinking at first I forgot something I flipped my bag around to see what was missing. "Okay, this has been bugging me for a while, but I know you from somewhere right?" Apparently my guess was dead on.

"I don't think so."

"Really, because I swear I have seen you somewhere but I just can't place it," she desperately looks for something to connect this lost memory.

"AKA party, some other party, pre-req class?" I ask, seeing if that sparks an idea.

"AKA? I've never been to a party but I feel like that is something." She just looks at me as if she is waiting for me to tell her where she knows me. It won't happen. Besides this class I have never seen her before. We just stand for a few minutes in silence as she awkwardly stares at me. If she weren't cute I would have left by now.

Finally the waiting become tedious and my patience grows thin. "Well, maybe you will figure it out later." I turn to leave as I feel her tug at my shirt.

"Arnold Billson!" she exclaims. I am taken aback and I stop breathing. It's been three days I haven't thought of that guy and now she brought him back to my mind. I get angry at her for bringing back his memory. "Yeah, I remember now, he talked about you a few times I think. He's your roommate right?"

"He was," I say as sadness takes over the anger.

"Was, did he transfer somewhere?" she asks.

I pause and wipe my mouth and look up to the sky for a second. "Ah, yeah. Kind of, ah, he died." There is silence, as her eyes open wide much like a deer's right before the semi hits it. I know she doesn't know what to say. "He went peacefully," I say, lying to her. It's the best thing to do. If I didn't, she would just cry.

"What happened?" she asks.

"His heart gave out." It's not fully a lie I guess, his heart did stop, and it gives him a little more dignity than choking on his own vomit.

"I'm so sorry," she says as she gives me a hug. Her tight embrace feels amazing against my body.

"Thanks. It sucks not having him around anymore."

"He talked about you a lot. You two must have been really close." I give her a nod. "Yeah he once suggested I..." she pauses and strokes her fingers through her hair. "Never mind, I will see you later okay? Bye"

"Bye."

I got back to the frat house late at night and I could hear some of the brothers screaming and yelling at each other.

"I'm going to freaking shoot you in your face," screamed one.

"Yeah, you want to but you ain't gonna," screamed another.

I follow the screams and find a bunch of the brothers in a room playing some first player shooter game. Unaware of my presence I watch as they play on. They swear and threaten each other throughout the game and when it's done the victor lets out a mighty warrior scream.

Slowly one by one they turn to see me standing in the doorway watching them play.

"Hey Tyler," says Jerry as if he was talking to a small child. "What's up?"

"Nothing," I respond.

There is a long pause as the three others in the room wait for Jerry to say something again. As if, because he spoke first, he is in charge of speaking the rest of the time. "Would you like to play a game?" he asks.

"Nah, I'm good." I can see their relief. Leaving the doorway and heading down the hall I can hear the screams begin again. They didn't want me to join them, they were just trying to be nice. It's freaking annoying the way they treat me here. It's like they think I am this fragile child that might snap and break down crying or start killing people. I can't stand it. I don't know if it's the memories or the way they look at me. I have to leave, I don't know where, I just need to find somewhere new.

Chapter 14

My life is filled with pain and happiness. Living at the frat house was destroying my soul. Every second I was there I was thinking of Arnold, his memory was destroying my life. There would be days I would cry myself to sleep. The only happiness I have is with Rebecca. She became my friend, and then that night after our final presentation, my girlfriend.

The group goes out to celebrate at this bar in town. After a few drinks we find ourselves closer and closer to each other. We talk for hours as the members of our group left. She came with Ashley, the other girl in our group, but leaves with me.

Too drunk to drive, we hail a cab, and instead of taking her to my place or hers, we have the cabbie drop us off near the beach. It was like something out of a chick flick. I chase her on the beach and when I finally catch her we share a deep kiss as we fall to the sand.

The next morning we wake on that beach half dressed. The looks we got from those parents who brought their kids to the beach early that day! We don't care. It takes us an hour to get to her apartment, and two hours for me to leave. From there I only have to walk twenty minutes to the frat house. Who knew that the love of my life was so close all this time?

I am happier than any drug or drink had ever made me, but as soon as I step in that frat house I get hit with a wave of depression. It's like someone's erased my memories of my night with Rebecca. I become sadder with each step to my room. At the beach I felt everyone's eyes on me, but now I feel as if no one wants to make eye contact.

The moment I get into my room I start packing. I can't live here anymore, it hurts too much, and quickly I pack up everything I have. Half way through packing I realize my mistake. I have nowhere to go, and I can't go back home to Utah with Rebecca here. On top of that my car is still at the bar.

With my stuff scattered around my room in boxes or suitcases I head out to get my car. The moment I step out of that house the pain lifts from my shoulders and I start to think of Rebecca once more, free from any painful memory of Arnold.

The next day I get a text from Rebecca.

"Why aren't you here?" she asks.

"Where," I respond.

"My bed," adding a smiley face to the message.

I'm 100% sure that I just beat every running record in the world – it seemed like only seconds from when I saw her text to when I am wrapped in her arms on her bed. We lay in each other's arms all night unable to sleep while the other is next to us.

"What would you say is too fast?" she asks me.

"Ah, I don't know," I said, afraid to answer wrong.

Turning to me she put her hand on my chest and looked at me with a shocked and confused face. "No, not like that. Not at all like that," she said with a smile and then kissing me. "I mean, what would you say to moving in here?" I pause for a moment with what I can only guess from her expression is a blank stare. "You don't have to, to keep doing this," she points to herself and me. "I'm just saying my roommate is moving out and I need a roommate, and, well, I can't think of a better roommate." I give her a deep kiss and she pulls back. "So is that a yes?" she asks. I smile and kiss her again.

Rebecca is something out of a dream. Her long black hair falls on those tan shoulders. Her dark brown eyes trap me – once I look into them I can't get away.

Christmas at my house is pretty simple. We open presents Christmas day and have dinner with my grandparents. After that I don't really spend much time with my family. I just chill in my room texting Rebecca.

The week after Christmas, I return to the frat house and move my stuff into Rebecca's apartment.

Though I have my own room I rarely ever end up in there. This is what I was promised in a college experience, not all the crap teachers or bad roommates, but every night lying next to a girl. I know it's early but I can already tell that this is the girl that I am going to marry.

Rebecca has bettered my life. Our class schedule has me out early some days and her out late other days. When we're not naked I'm studying and find that I'm getting the best grades of my college career. But it's not all drinking and sex. I do have one class that is just a pain in the ass. I'm in an Entrepreneur class and for our entire grade, we have this group assignment. We have to come up with an idea and propose it in front of the class. Ten percent of the grade is based on the number of students willing to invest their imaginary money in our imaginary business.

I can understand the purpose of the assignment and class but that's for people who want to run their own businesses. I just want to get a job with good pay and some benefits. Really, a job where I sit at a desk and put people on hold for ten minutes before I answer their questions.

There's tension from the very start of this project. I don't know what it is, but there's something that is not right with this group. Our very first assignment for the group was to come up with three ideas for a business. It should have been easy, one good idea that we plan on doing and two other ideas just to complete the requirement.

The four of us sit in a study room for nearly two hours and fight over this. One guy Jeff is the problem and this girl Carly agrees with him the entire time, even though half the time he does not make any sense. The other girl, Amber, who is the "leader" of the group, is quiet but chimes in every so often trying to calm tempers.

We stay quiet after a ten minute yelling fit until I decide that I want to get home to Rebecca.

"Listen, we have our idea," I say, my hand firmly resting behind my head. "We are going to open a coffee shop across the street from the college right?" Amber nods, while Jeff glares, and then Carly snarls when she sees Jeff's reaction. "We don't need to fight about this at all. We are just wasting time. Let's just say our other ideas are to start an outdoor movie theater and a clothing line. They sound like real ideas and then we can focus on the coffee shop."

"We are not doing a movie theater or a clothing line. That's just stupid," says Jeff, slamming his hand on the table.

"I agree, they just don't make sense," Carly says, just to agree with Jeff.

"They don't need to make sense, we just need two other ideas. You are making this assignment harder then its suppose to be," I say to Jeff.

"You don't freaking care about this assignment, you are going to destroy my chances of getting into the masters program," Jeff yells at me. He crosses his arms across his chest and sits up tall in his chair as if he is trying to intimidate me.

"What the hell are you talking about?" I say. "We have to write a one paragraph proposal for three ideas. Rank them in the order that we like and then we pick one of our ideas. And let's get one thing straight. THIS ISN'T REAL!" I say raising my voice. "We are not actually going to start a business so there isn't any real risk. Hell, this part of the assignment is worth five points. That's 1% of the total grade. Even if we fail, guess what? We can still get a 99%. So lets just write three paragraphs and be done!"

Jeff looks at me as he slowly takes his hands from under his arms and puts his clenched hands on the table. I look around the room and as I turn back to Jeff he is still looking at me with a fierce stare. He stands up and looks down at me. His face begins to turn red as I prepare myself for what I expect will be a failed attempt to attack me.

"Screw this!" he says grabbing his bag. "You do it." Jeff storms out of the study room, punching the door loudly to open it. The three of us are silent as he leaves, half expecting him to come back.

Carly, realizing first that Jeff isn't coming back stands up and picks up her binder and purse and looks at me and Amber. "You know he's right, you two aren't taking this seriously. We should listen to Jeff. He would get us a good grade," she says leaving in a huff. She tries to act like Jeff but her exit isn't as dramatic as she hoped for.

I turn to Amber, who seems just as confused as me. "I wasn't in the wrong, right?"

"I can understand why he wants to make sure we do well on this project but I don't understand his attitude," she says. "Let's just write three solid paragraphs and go home.

It takes us five minutes to finish the three paragraphs, even with a few rewrites, and then go our separate ways. I walk to school these days. Parking passes are nearly $500, and I need the walk so that I'm not angry when I get home to Rebecca.

When I get back, Rebecca is quiet. Usually when one of us gets back the other rushes to see the other, but this time she just sits on the couch watching some reality show.

"Hey babe," I say, thinking that she didn't hear me come in. "Becky?" Again she ignores me. I drop my bag and make my way to the couch and sit down next to her. I go to put my arm around her but as my arm gets close she moves farther away from me. "What's wrong?"

"Where were you?"

"I was with my entrepreneur group."

"You said you would be home over an hour ago," she says, staring at me as if I had insulted her in some way.

"I thought I was, but this tool in our group was being an idiot and made us stay there longer."

"You could have called," she says, her face becoming more sad than mad.

"I'm sorry I will call next time," I say softly, rubbing her arm hoping to get a smile out of her. "You look beautiful."

She gives me a slight smile but then her face goes back to being sad. "I made you dinner, it's in the fridge."

"Thanks babe, but I'm not really hungry," I say getting closer to her.

"I worked hard making you lasagna."

"I mean, I have something else in mind." I lean over and kiss her pouting lips, and let her lead me to her room.

That day won't be the last time that my group causes problems for Rebecca and me. It was like Jeff and Carly have this plan to destroy our relationship, even though I never said I was even in one. Per the class requirement we meet once a week, that day annoyingly being Thursday, to go over details of the project and divide the work. Thursdays used to be a day to let loose and relax from the stress of college, but now it has become a day I loathe and wish I could sleep through. Most nights the group meetings go long and I would either be too tired to go out drinking with Rebecca, or Rebecca's mad that I'm so late and she refuses to go out.

I take on more work in the group in hopes that our Thursday meetings would be shorter, but somehow Jeff finds something to bitch about. Amber is the smart one in the group. She's the only one of us that has a job, and because of that she is responsible for editing our work. That way she doesn't have to do research or anything, she just makes sure we don't sound like illiterate Neanderthals when we turn in our paper.

Halfway through the year we have a meeting with a real estate agent to learn about contracts, and the cost of renting versus buying a building across the street from the school. Jeff and Carly are supposed to go and meet with this agent but twenty minutes before, I get a call from Amber telling me that they can't make it asking me to go instead. I tell Amber that I have a date but she doesn't know if we'll get another chance to meet with the agent. Regretfully I agree and call Rebecca. I don't reach her but her voice mail and I tell her that I have to push back our date an hour.

I meet the agent, unprepared, and ask him all the questions I can think of that we might need to know. The agent can see that I'm unprepared but doesn't comment on it. He does answer the questions very quickly, and I have to ask multiple follow-up questions to his very short, vague answers.

When I get home I take Rebecca out but there's tension the entire night. With each word I speak, I feel like I am taking a chance that I will set off an explosion of anger. When we get back home, she goes to her room without a kiss goodnight or even just the words. I am in the doghouse because of that stupid group.

Sleeping in my bed, something I hadn't done in a long time, I realize how uncomfortable it is. No wonder we never spent a night here. Struggling to sleep for hours, I go out to sleep on the couch. It isn't comfortable either but the slight smell of Rebecca's perfume is enough to get me to sleep. I wake with the sun but when I go to her room she is already gone. I send her a dozen red long stemmed roses to her work, I hope that it will be enough for her to forgive me for my stupid group.

Two weeks later we get our papers back from the teacher on meeting with the real estate agent. Jeff is handed the paper and shows the grade over his shoulder. 73%.

"Nice job," Jeff says to me.

"You don't like it? Well, next time do your damn job so I don't have to do it," I say back, not wanting to be blamed for a grade that wasn't my responsibility.

The teacher hearing our short anger filled conversation asked to speak to us after class. Amber is not there so it is just Jeff, Carly, and me waiting after class.

"So what's the problem here?" asked Professor Mason. He is an old man but is in better shape then anyone else his age. He wears a ring with some military symbol on it, and stands like a statue. His voice is deep and powerful and has a strength that makes you feel weak.

"I'm mad that Tyler messed up the paper. If we fail it's his fault," says Jeff, while Carly nods in agreement. It's like Carly doesn't understand anything and just agrees with Jeff because he screams the most. She probably just wants to be on his good side so he doesn't turn on her.

"Where's your other member," asks Professor Mason.

"I don't know," I say.

"Your group should be working on these papers together. It is a group project not only designed to help your learning but to help you to become more efficient in a group."

"Yeah, but he decided to do the paper on his own, not asking for any of our help," says Jeff.

"That's bullshit," I cut in before he can say anything else.

"Hey!" Professor yells. "Swearing of any kind is not permitted in my class room. Swearing is just a tool for idiots with a weak vocabulary."

"Sorry, but that assignment was their responsibility and they canceled at the last second, making me do it. They did not send me any question or notes on what to ask for the paper so I had to go in blind. Then I wrote the paper on what I learned and then submitted it the next day," I tell him, hoping he sees my point.

"You should have worked together on this project," he says looking at me. "I can't change your grade but if you do not work as a team your grade is going to reflect it. Now if you excuse me, I have a meeting to get to." With that he leaves the three of us alone in the classroom.

Jeff just stares at me and I can tell he is just cussing me out in his head. "Just do your work," I say and I make my way out of the classroom.

With only a month left in school, I try just to get by. I do my work and suffer through our meetings, which become more frequent as the school year comes to an end. This group has put a strain on Rebecca's and my relationship I know, but I need to pass this class. After finals things will get a lot better and we will go back to what it use to be. I do miss her bed.

Chapter 15

I'm standing outside the classroom, my hand behind my back to hide my nervousness. The tie around my neck seems to be growing tighter as the seconds go by, a smooth layer of sweat covers my skin under this black suit. I look at Jeff who glares at me. He knows I know that if we do not pass there will be punches thrown. The thing he just can't seem to comprehend is that I will knock him out. A part of me wants to fail just so that I can punch him and claim it was self-defense. If we can get half the class to consider our coffee shop a good investment we will pass the class. If not, we will fail the class. So much of our grade is based on other students. The idea that other students have so much control over our grade is dumbfounding.

The door opens and Professor Mason waves us back into the classroom. We stand in front of the class in suspense as we wait for the teacher to speak. The class gives us no clues about what may be our final grade. It is the last day and we are the last group. After two weeks of presentations, everyone is tired of listening to ideas that most of them think are a waste of time. There is one guy in the back looking down at his lap, most likely texting, and a girl passing notes to her friend, most likely saying how stupid this part of the class is.

Professor Mason clears his throat and takes his place in the center of the room right in front of a guy who obviously looks a tad frightened by the Professor's close proximity to him. I can feel the nervous energy from the other students waiting for the professor to tell us how our groups did. "Okay I want to thank the class for being honest about whether they would or would not want to invest in the proposals from your fellow students. Congratulations team, about 60% of the students thought your proposal is worthy of investment."

Sixty percent of the students didn't want to be a-holes that failed four people in the class is more like it, and 40% of the students are a-holes who enjoy having the power to destroy someone's grade. We take our seats as we listen to the professor say some pointless crap about the class and how it will help our future, and yada yada yada. He releases us and there is a simultaneous exhale from the entire class.

Walking out of the classroom in a slight rush, Jeff blocks the exit and I am ready to fight. I clench my fist, ready to swing at first movement.

"Listen I know that things weren't always easy but it's done. So yeah. Good job," he says to me. He reaches out his hand and I shake it but I feel like I just sealed my fate in hell by shaking hands with this devil.

I watch as he and Carly walk down the hall, right before they leave the building I see her grab his hand. No wonder that moron always agreed with him.

Another year done and one semester left before I graduate from dealing with stupid people like Jeff. The longer I spend at this school the more I realize that college is just supposed to encourage you to get out.

Getting back to Rebecca's and my place, I quickly shed my business suit and drop each piece around the room. Rebecca isn't here but she should be soon. Wanting to celebrate with her when she gets back, I go to the bathroom and prepare for her arrival.

I turn on the shower and sit on the toilet. Knowing that I won't be leaving the seat for a while I start reading one of Rebecca's magazines to help kill time. Basic female magazines about make-up and crap, but when you are taking a crap it's easy to be interested in this stuff. Reaching to put the magazine back on the counter I miss my target and it falls into the trash. As I pull it out something catches my eye. At first glance I think a thermometer had been dropped in the trash but on closer examination I discover what it really is.

No wonder she had been so distant the last couple weeks. She's pregnant! We are having a kid, and she doesn't know how I'll react. I quickly lock up from the stick at the plain white wall. "How do I act?" I say out loud. Marriage and kids aren't something I haven't thought of, but, I mean, I was more thinking a few years down the road after college and when I have a job. I have another semester of college left and she graduates after this semester but she can't work when the kid is born. I mean, it's possible that she has the kid and she quits her job and I would have a job and with my degree I should make good enough money to support both a baby and us. But, a baby.

Taking a quick shower, I get dressed and wait for her to return from wherever she is. With time my shaking hands calm and the fear leaves my body. I sit in silence at the kitchen table ready for her to walk through that door.

The door opens and Rebecca walks in. Her hair is messy and she is in her gym clothes. She looks like she hasn't slept in days, but I understand the stress she is going through – if I am scared she must be terrified. Startled by my presence as if she didn't expect to see me she looks and me and then at the pregnancy test in front of me. "Where did you find that?" she says in a panic as if I had a gun pointed at her.

"It was in the trash," I say, showing her my hands are empty in hopes it will calm her down.

"You shouldn't have done that," she says, starting to pace back and forth. I stand up and go to comfort her but the closer I get the farther she gets away from me. I stop, not knowing what to do, and wait for her to speak. "Tyler I," she pauses and wipes the tears that are now falling down her face. "I can't deal with this right now." I take another step towards her and she quickly holds up her hand for me to stop. "No! No! I need some time." She goes to the garage and slams the door hard behind her. I hear the squeal of the tires as she drives away.

I quickly text her, letting her know that I'm not angry but I get no response. She must think that I can't handle this. I need to show her that I can, and we can do this together. For hours I wait for her to return but she doesn't. Finally I get a text back from her. "Going home for the night. Be back tomorrow." I think about driving up to see her but decide she needs some time alone.

The next morning I drive to the mall and walk around trying to clear my head. There is only one way to keep Rebecca and make her realize that I'm ready for this.

I buy a diamond ring from the jewelers. It's nothing flashy but it will serve its purpose. Though it's small, I will be paying off this ring for years. I stop by the florist and pick up a dozen red roses. As soon as I get back to the apartment I start cleaning as fast as I can. I don't know when she will return so I hurry. Every so often I look outside the balcony to see if she is coming.

I take a quick shower and get into that black suit once more. My right leg crossed over the other, I nervously wait for her to return. Leg shaking I go over what I'm going to say in my head for hours. After what seems like an eternity, I hear the garage door open. Rising to my feet I turn on some slow music and with flowers and ring in hand I watch for that door to open.

Rebecca walks in startled by what she sees. She has never looked more beautiful to me.

"Hi," I say trying to stop smiling so that I can continue.

"Tyler listen," she says as I walk up to her.

"Wait let me say something first," I say cutting her off. "I know why you are nervous but you don't have to worry. I love you and I know that we can do this. It will be hard but I know we can do it." I hand her the flowers and drop to a knee. Pulling up the ring I look at her eyes as they begin to water. "Rebecca will you marry me?" I open the box to show her the ring.

She puts the flowers on the table and tries to wipe the tears from her eyes. "No."

My heart feels like it drops out of my body, my smile vanishes and I am at a loss for words. I try to talk but can only manage a small mumble. "W-why?"

"I just can't." She walks around me and goes to her room. Stuck still on my knee for a moment, I struggle to my feet and follow her.

"What do you mean you can't? We can do this, I know we can."

"No we can't," she says refusing to look at me.

"Did you lose the baby?" I ask, nervous to hear the answer.

"No. I still have the baby," she says.

"Then it will be fine. You can get a job for a few months as I finish school, and then by the time you have the baby I will graduate and I will work and you can stay home and take care of our baby." I walk over to her and grab her shoulders holding her close to me. She refuses to look at me but I'm willing to wait. "I know this is sudden and not according to anyone's plans but I knew from our first kiss that you were the one I was going to marry. I love you."

She turns her head and looks at me. "It's not yours." My body begins to shake and my heartbeat and breathing stops. Slowly I back away from her as my skin becomes cold.

"W-w-what do..." I stutter, unable to complete the sentence.

"It's not yours." She starts to pack as my eyes lose focus of everything in the room, the ring still in my hand. There is silence as she continues to pack something into a suitcase.

"Why?" I say in a dismal voice.

"We were on the verge of breaking up, and you were never here, and you were always calling off our dates," she says quickly throwing things violently into the suitcase.

"But...but," I try to start before being cut off by her.

"You weren't there for me."

"Bullshit!" I scream finding my voice. "You freaking cheated on me and you're blaming me for your whoring around."

"Don't put this on me," she says.

"Why not? You're putting it on me and I'm not the one screwing around like a slut."

"This is what drove us away."

"What the hell are you talking about? You being a slut drove you away from me, I did nothing! I loved you and you cheated on me."

"Stop it!"

"How long?"

"How long what," she asks as she starts to cry.

"How long did you cheat on me?"

"A month," she says zipping-up her suitcase and pulling it off the bed. "I'll send someone else to get the rest of my stuff." She makes her way to the door and I follow as I watch her walk out to the garage.

I hastily follow her out and get in front of her car so she can't leave, raising my hands up to show I'm blocking her. She releases go of the brake and rolls forward hoping that I'll move but I won't move.

"Get out of the way," she yells rolling down the window.

"Who," I yell back.

"What?"

"Who the hell did you screw?"

She looks at me and slams her hand on the wheel. "Jack Dorn."

My hands drop and I move out of her way. Not wanting to stay a second more, she speeds out of the apartment complex. I stand there still as I see a woman standing on he balcony. Her face looks sympathetic, as our screams were loud enough for her to hear. I nod at her and walk back into the apartment.

Going to the kitchen I open the freezer and pull out a half empty vodka bottle. I close the door and fall back against the fridge and then down to the ground. I unscrew the top and start drinking. Rapidly I chug down half of what was left in the bottle. Tears running down my face I start to cry like a baby. Loud and filled with pain I slam my empty hand on the ground. I finish the bottle and throw it towards a picture of Rebecca and me on a bookshelf. I stumble across the room and crawl over to the bookshelf. Pulling myself up, I pick up the picture of us at the beach. We look so happy in this picture. A tear falls down my face but the tears become heated and I start to slam the picture violently against the wall, busting the glass and then frame. I pull out the picture as blood begins to cover my face. Tearing the picture in half I rush to the kitchen nearly falling over. I open up every drawer pulling one completely out searching for a lighter. Finding the lighter I watch as her picture burns. "Wish this was, you slut," I say as the fire engulfs her.

I wake up to the sound of voices. My head feels like it has be run over by a truck, and my eyes burn while my vision is blurry. I can see figures in the apartment but I can't make them out. When my vision finally clears I see two men in front of me. Jumping to my feet I grab a knife on the counter as the jump back in fear. "Who the hell are you?" I scream.

The two men take a few steps back and put their hands up. One of the men, a tall guy with long blonde hair looks at me scared, "Rebecca asked us to pick up her stuff." He fumbles in is pocket quickly pulling out a key attached to a star keychain. "See," he says his hand shaking.

I lower the knife but the two men are still startled and scared that I may use the knife on them.

"Listen," says the other man, who has a long thin beard and thick rimmed glasses. "We are just going to grab her stuff and leave. That's it, okay? We don't want any trouble."

With the knife still in my hand I go over to the cabinet and pull out a bottle of tequila. "Hurry the hell up." I walk over to the couch, sit down, and start drinking. For the next half hour they grab things out of her room.

"That's it," calls out the man with the beard.

"Hey!" I yell, the knife firmly in my hand. The two men stop as if they are frozen in their shoes. "Either of you know a Jack Dorn?"

The two look at each other and nervously look back at me. "N-no," says the longhaired one. There is a slight pause before he speaks again. "Why?"

"Just wouldn't mind meeting the guy." I begin to play with the knife in my hand. The longhaired man pushes his friend towards the door and the two quickly leave.

Chapter 16

I have gained about 20 pounds this summer. There's no point in staying in shape when the love of your life cuts out your heart. I spend my days in the same apartment we once shared or at the school working my pointless job to kill the hours in the day I'm not drunk.

The school has royally screwed me once more. I was supposed to graduate this fall but thanks to them accepting more students then they can handle I'm forced to stay here for another semester and shell out another 20 grand just to get that stupid piece of paper. Schools are purposely allowing too many students to enroll, forcing them to struggle to get into classes. My only chance of actually graduating in the fall is to crash the class I need, but classrooms are so overpopulated it never works. I think I have crashed six classes in the last four years and only got into one, and that was some English class I didn't even need for my major, just something to bring my GPA up.

There is a new guy living in the tramp's room. His name is Sid, he is a sophomore at the same school. He is so annoying, he is always yelling at me for drinking too much and not cleaning up after myself. I don't drink too much and if I leave out a bottle he freaks. If he really cares that much he can just take it to the trash himself. Who cares? In five months hopefully I will be out of here. If not, well, it's going to be a long year for that prude.

Sitting at the desk at the Student Center a day before the school year starts, I watch movies online. One of the most helpful tools I have learned in college is how to download shows. All the shows I miss because I don't want to pay an extra $40 a month I now get for free. Hell, shows should be free online anyways with all the advertisements they force me to watch. These last two weeks of work have be the best I have had here. Joel and I do about ten minutes of filing to prepare for this next semester and then we watch six hours of shows and movies, and the school pays us for this crap.

Right in the middle of this pirate-based drama that we started to get into I get a call from my mom. I quickly sent it to voicemail and not ten seconds later she calls again, once more I send it to voicemail. Finally on the third time I answer the phone.

"Mom, I can't talk I'm at work," I say already prepared to hang up.

"We need to talk," says my father.

"Why are you on Mom's phone?" I ask confused.

"It's important. Can you talk?"

"Yeah, hold on," I pull the phone from my ear and cover it so my father can't hear me. "Joel pause it, I got to talk to my father."

"Okay, hurry up this is the episode we find out if the queen's child is Captain Patter's," he says, stuffing his mouth with popcorn.

I walk out of the Student Center and bring the phone back to my ear. "Okay I'm outside. What's up?" I can hear my mom crying on the other end. At first thought I think someone has died.

"Tyler, we are calling to let you know that your mother and I won't be able to pay for half your college like we promised," my father says to me. My body freezes and I feel a cold child run down to my toes. "Tyler?"

"What do you mean you won't be able to pay...you said...why?" I start to dig my nails into the top of my skull.

"Your mother and I met this property developer who had a plan to build a new community. For a small investment we would share 50% of the profits." He pauses and I hear my Mom's cries even more clearly. "It was a scam. He took everything."

"What do you mean everything?" I ask.

"We're wiped out. We have to sell the house."

"What the hell? Didn't you check this guy out before he took you for everything?"

"He had all the right documents..." he starts before I cut him off.

"How can you be so stupid?"

"Hey, do not disrespect me boy."

"Disrespect? You have to respect someone first to do that. You forced me to go to college and now you are telling me the bill is on me? You screwed me! I will be paying this debt off for the next 30 years you asshole."

"Tyler!"

"Go to hell!" With that I hang up the phone. Rage still building, I slam my phone into the ground, breaking it into a hundred pieces. I stamp my feet hard into the ground towards the building. Scratching my nails down the walls I can feel a few of my nails bending backwards. I start to punch the wall like a punching bag trying to my anger out of my system, until my hands are bruised and bloody.

Pulling open the door I walk back into the Student Center, my hands feeling the pain of my parents' mistake.

"Dude, what the hell?" says Joel seeing my bloody knuckles. He hands me a couple paper towels from under the desk and I wrap them up. "You need ice or something?"

"Nah, I'm good." I say waving him off with my towel wrapped hand.

"What happened?" he asks, probably thinking that someone attacked me.

"Bad phone call with my father." I proceed to tell him the story and his face is filled with disbelief and sadness for me. As I speak I look for a miracle and hope Joel is some rich guy's son and will solve all my problems. However, that is not the case and I leave early to get my hands properly bandaged.

We don't have aspirin or anything like that but some tequila does the job. I have trouble opening and closing my hands so it takes two tries to get the bottle to my lips. Sid doesn't even bother to ask what happened to my hands when he gets back to the apartment. I take the next day off, saying I need to heal, but I just want to drink until the pain goes away. But it doesn't, no matter how much I drink.

School starts and I go to crash the class. I get there 15 minutes before class starts and the room is filled to the brim with students. There are about 40 people in the class and another 20 around the walls of the classroom. The teacher walks in and is stunned to see so many people in her classroom.

"Hello, I see we have a lot of people crashing so if you are not already scheduled in this class please give a seat to someone already in the class," she says, as she makes her way to the front of the class. A few people get up and the seats are quickly taken. I make my way to the front following her so I can speak to her.

"Hi, my name is Tyler…" I start.

"I will deal with crashers after class, please just wait," she says pointing me back to the wall. So I stand at the wall for the next two hours as she calls the roll, goes over the class curriculum, and then goes over the first assignment. She would have talked for another hour if she didn't see that clock. "Now, is there anyone who thinks that they want to drop this class?" she asks looking around for volunteers. "No? Okay. I am sorry but no crashers will be allowed." A loud moan of grief travels around the room. "I'm sorry but we are filled up and we don't want the Fire Marshal on our case."

She releases the class and nearly two dozen walk out disappointed that the teacher wasted their time. Instead of following the zombies, I make my way to the front once more to speak with her.

"Excuse me Professor, I was wondering if there was anyway I can change your mind about letting in crashers," I ask in my most desperate voice.

"I'm sorry but where would I put you? All the desks are filled. You will just need to take it next semester." She doesn't care.

"Here's the thing, I need this one last class to graduate this semester or else I will have to come back in the spring and pay another $20,000. I don't mind if I just stand against the wall."

"We can't allow you to do that," she says giving me a lame smile.

"Well, I bet at least one person a day won't be here each class so there will be a seat available."

"But everyone is here for test day."

"Well, I can take the test up front."

"Then I won't have a seat," she says, picking up her book and binder she brought with her and starts heading out.

I follow her desperate for her to change her mind. "Here's the thing. I was signed up for this class and a stupid computer error dropped me." It didn't happen but I have heard of it happening before so why not use it.

"That's too bad. You should talk to Registration about that."

"I did and they told me that they couldn't do anything so I should just crash." Now I'm pretty much begging.

"Sorry, better luck next time," she gives me another pointless smile and walks away. If I wasn't afraid that she would be my teacher next semester I would have cussed her out right there.

I go home thinking maybe it is best just to drop out now before I spend any more money. I've already paid for this semester before the parents decided to drop a giant F-U on me. There is no point in dropping out now when I'm so close to that stupid piece of paper that is suppose to get me a high paying job and whatnot. I don't even know how much I'm going to pay in student loans at the end of all this.

Chapter 17

I saw Rebecca today. She was at the grocery store. She looks especially fat now. She's probably getting pretty close now to popping out that little bastard. I wonder if she will ever tell that kid about what a whore their mother is. I feel bad for saying that for a moment but I get over it and go back to loathing that thing.

I didn't plan to go out tonight, but after seeing Rebecca, I wanted to go out to drink. I go to the Brick House with some guys who also work at the Student Center. The Brick House is just a converted warehouse that they turned into a club. It's nothing special but it's easy to get to and the bartenders are generous with the liquor. They play dubstep at ear piercing levels so you don't have to waste your time talking to people.

After about an hour, or six drinks, of ruining my hearing I decided I am ready to leave. I motion to the guys that I am leaving. Going around I high five everyone to be nice and then make my way through the dance floor to the exit. The dance floor swarms with drunken sweaty people thinking they can dance. If I wasn't being pushed from side to side I was getting slapped in the face with hair.

Suddenly I feel someone touching my butt. Thinking it was someone trying to steal my wallet, I grab the thief's hand. Prepared to punch the idiot in the face I turn, fist clenched, to see my hand clutching a redhead's arm.

She is scared, thinking that I am going to hit her, and if she didn't have such long hair I would have swung my fist at her not seeing she was a girl. I try to apologize over the music but the sound from my mouth can't reach her ears. This girl must be forgiving. I guess she understand what I must have thought, because moments after, she starts dancing. Her green eyes hypnotize me and I lose control of my body. Grabbing my hands she moves me around the dance floor, our bodies getting closer and closer with each beat of the bass. That black dress feels good against me. Moving like a snake on my body she has me in her coils. She turns quickly around and pulls my head down towards her. At first I think we are going to kiss but then she turns my head and sticks her tongue in my ear. Slowly she walks away as I watch thinking she was done with me, but then she turns and with one finger signals me to follow.

We leave the club and get into a cab.

"Your place," she says, as she starts to kiss my neck.

I give the cab my address and a look to tell him to hurry. In the cab she can't keep her hands off me. The cab stops and I pay the fare and we go up to my apartment. I try to pull her to my room as fast as I can but she pulls me back towards the front. Thinking I ruined my shot by going to fast, I pause.

"You got anything to drink I here?" she asks.

I go over to the refrigerator and hold up wine and vodka. She points to the wine and I pour two glasses. She walks over to me and takes a glass out of my hand.

Giving me a kiss she stands close and whispers, "Get that vodka too."

I turn and grab the vodka and then she hands me the glass of wine. She drinks the wine like a shot so I do the same. Turning towards my bedroom she unzips her short mini skirt and walks in. Leaving the vodka, I walk in after her.

The next morning I wake up naked in my bed, my head is hurting and I feel nauseated. The room won't stop spinning and I feel like I'm still drunk from last night. I lift my body up but quickly fall back to the mattress. Turning my head I see that the girl is gone. The last thing I remember was that tattoo on her back that her dress had covered. It was a tree, or a river. I can't remember. Slowly I try to remember what had happened last night.

Went to the club. Tried to leave. Met girl. Danced with that girl. Left with that girl. Came here. Went to my room. Woke up. What happened in between going to my room and waking up?

Why can't I remember? How much did I have to drink? This is something I don't want to forget. She was the hottest thing I have ever done and now I can't remember it. Why didn't she stay, or did I ask her to leave? I put on some shorts and see if she left a note in the kitchen or something. No letter. No note. How could I not get her number? Well obviously I must have had better things to do then find out her life story.

I shower and get dressed and go to work. My head is still pounding and my vision and mind still fuzzy. I do less then I usually do.

BAM! The sound of Joel slamming a book on my desk rings through my ears. My body jolts to his enjoyment.

"Whoa! Sorry dude, didn't mean to scare you that much," he says, with a stupid smile on his face. "Late night?"

Rubbing the sleep out of my eyes, I push my hands through my hair. "Yeah, not the best morning though."

"Hey, I'm going to get an early lunch, you coming?" he asks, tapping me on the shoulder. The force from just a tap on the shoulder shakes my brain within my skull.

Right as I'm about to say no, the phone rings. "Yeah," I say so I don't have to answer the phone. He doesn't expect me to pick up the phone and we head to his car. We drive to The Sombrero right as the lunch rush starts. After fifteen minutes of waiting in line and hoping that Joel just wants food and not conversation, we finally make it up to the front. I order my food but when I go to pay I notice my wallet is not in my pants.

"Joel, can I borrow $10?" I ask turning to him.

"Yeah why?" he asks as he hands me the money.

"I must have left it in my other jeans." I hand the money to the cashier and find a seat. I'm tortured by Joel and his questions about last night. He is a few years older than me yet he acts like a little brother amazed by what his big brother does. Thinking that there would be no relief, our food finally arrives. Joel's attention quickly changes to his tacos, and I devour my carne asada burrito. Nothing makes a hangover better than a carne asada burrito with avocado and red peppers.

After work I go home and instantly fall asleep. Sid is never around here anymore, except for when he comes back to sleep. It's nice to pretty much have the apartment to myself. Sid's a tool anyway. He is always complaining to me about little things I do and is always in a bad mood. It's like, come on dude, you're having a bad day, don't put it on me.

After my nap I look around my room but can't find my wallet. I clean my room in the first time in a year in hopes it's hiding somewhere, but to no avail. Thinking I left it in the cab, I call the company and they say they'll get back to me. Seconds after hanging up with the cab company, I get a call telling me where my wallet is, with the redhead from the other night. Apparently she thought I should pay for a shopping spree. If she hadn't gone over my limit, I would have no idea until I got my bill. The good news is that I won't be charged. The bad news is that I lost something like $50 in cash another $100 in gift cards and whatever it's going to cost to replace all the other crap in that wallet.

The next week I realized that I am 100% sure that that redhead and me had sex, as the proof starts to emanate from my balls. I start to get a red rash that itches at first and then slowly blisters appeared that burst every so often. I have to go to the doctor and be humiliated as he tells me that I should have been more careful.

He gives me a prescription that barely does anything to help It takes some of the pain away but not all and the red marks stay. If I miss taking the pills and putting on the cream I was prescribed, it flares up like I'm wearing barbed wired underwear.

Of course the next girl I bring home sees the markings and runs scared. Even though I tell her I'm not contagious, she runs. Now I either have to date a girl who already has herpes too, or just not say anything and make sure to keep the lights off.

College is more ninja training then anything else. With each passing year I learn to sneak and move without the teachers noticing. Professors give tests that they don't even create and expect us to pass them, so I feel no shame when I cheat. Whether it is the simple tactic of writing definitions on your shoe, or a well placed cell phone, I find a way to pass their tests.

One semester to go, one class to finish, and then I'm done with this corrupt system.

Chapter 18

What a waste. Problem Analysis and Implementation, also known as Business 425. A single class to get that stupid degree costs me $15,000. In what world is it legal to charge someone such an immense amount? I'm paying $500 a day for a class that I have to share with 200 other students for a teacher that spends the day reading slides. Not only are they slides but also they are slides that he didn't even make himself. He is such a lazy professor that he doesn't bother copying and pasting the slides but use the slides that came with the teacher's copy of the book. Obviously this class is worth $15,000.

I have picked up more hours at the Student Center. At first I thought it would be a good idea to start chipping away at that debt that I will have when I graduate, but now I see that there is no point. $8.75 won't even make a dent in the $200,000 plus that I will owe that stupid lending company.

Joel has been trying to convince me to get a job here but there is no way in hell I want to be stuck like him. The pay's crap and I'd have to be here, with him. Each time I tell him that he is the only good reason to stay there, but that's just to get him to shut up and not cause issues during my last three months here.

The only time I have talked to Sid this semester was when he told me that he was going to move out at the end of the year. I put on the act of the sad roommate but I could care less. When I graduate, I'm getting the hell out of this city. Maybe I'll move up to Los Angeles and get a place up there. I can find a job that pays $35,000 with decent promotion opportunities.

In Business 425 I get my first paper back. C-. Once again another paper with a grade with no reason why I deserve that grade. After class I go to the front to talk to the professor about my grade.

He is a fat man in a suit that he must have had for a long time. It is faded and worn. He has thick glasses and is a heavy breather. I could have overlooked the breathing but the pathetic attempt at a comb over drove me crazy.

"Excuse me, Professor Hanover. I wanted to ask you about my paper." I point down at the paper in my hand.

"Really?" he says, as if he was confused by my request. "What's wrong?"

"Well, I got a 72% and wanted to know why it was so low. I feel like I followed the directions and think I came up with a well-written proposal for the company to initiate."

"You think so?" he says, signaling me to hand him my paper. I hand him the paper and he starts to hum as he quickly goes over it. When he reaches the final page he points down at the grade. "72%. That's not my handwriting. Must be Clare's. She's one of my teaching aides. I'm sorry I can't tell you why you got that grade." He hands me back the paper. "You should ask her." He grabs back my paper and writes down Clare's email address and then hands me the paper once more. "Here, email her and see what you were missing."

"Ah," I start confused, "can you take a look at it. I'm sure that she made a mistake."

"Sorry but I have full confidence in my T.A. You will just have to ask her and find out what you did wrong. Have a nice weekend," he says as he hurries to the exit so that I don't stop him again to continue the conversation.

I head to the library and email this "Clare" about what she found was wrong with my paper, hoping that she would meet with me and say she made a mistake and get the teacher to change my grade. I get an email from her saying that she would meet with me to discuss why she gave me such a low score.

The next day I wait in the library for Clare to show up. I sat there for 20 minutes just playing on my phone growing more irritated with each second that went by.

"Are you Tyler," a voice says behind me.

Finally this idiot shows up late. I turn expecting to see some ugly book worm but instead this hot blonde in a short shorts. "Ah, yeah," I say pleasantly surprised.

"Hi I'm Clare. Sorry that I'm late. There was an accident on the freeway," she says, a little out of breath.

"No worries. I was just playing on my phone."

"It's kind of busy in here. You want to see if we can find an open study room?"

"Yeah."

We get in the elevator and without a word spoken between us, we look for an open room. Of course my mind goes to that fantasy. Finally we find one and she waves me in.

"Okay, so let's see it," she says.

"Huh," I respond.

"Your paper. I need to see your paper."

"Oh yeah." I reach in my bag and hand her my paper.

She rereads the entire paper, pushing her finger into the paper every so often as if to be making mental notes as she runs her finger back and forth along the page, nodding her head to agree or disagree for every paragraph.

"All right," she says, putting down the paper. "72% was the right grade."

"What?" I say. "What was wrong with it?"

"Well a lot of things. Honestly it was a fairly generous grading.   Besides some grammatical errors, your idea of what the company should do was vague and would confuse the client. You need to be clearer.   Clients are going to read through these things quickly and need straightforward suggestions."

"The paper had to be ten pages though." I say puzzled.

"Well, yes but it's more important to have a good paper than the right amount of pages."

"But Professor Hanover said that it had to be at least ten pages. I mean, I could have been more direct in like eight but then I wouldn't hit the requirement."

"You should write ten, but don't add so much fluff to get there."

The hypocrisy of what she was saying was driving me insane. Write ten but don't write ten, but you have to write ten. I clench my toes so she doesn't see my anger. "So how would you suggest I get a better grade? I mean we only have the final left and my grade is borderline right now and if I don't pass I have to take this class another freaking time."

"Well you could study harder," she says.

That is the worst advice that I could hear, and not even the first time that I have heard it in this place. "I honestly think I'm doing the best I can. Is there any way that you could help me? I mean can you show me what I need to do for the final so I can study better or help me with the writing prompt?"

"That sounds too much like cheating and I think that would give you an advantage over your other classmates." She gets up but then sits down again. Staring at my face she smiles. "How desperate are you?"

"Very!" I say quickly. "This stupid school has already screwed me into wasting another semester here to take this one class, along with other crap they've done to me the other years I been here. I just want to pass and get out of here."

Clare puts her hands on the table, folding one over the other. "Here's the thing. I read your paper and, well, you can improve, but not much. You pretty much won't pass." My eyes open and I don't breathe for a moment. "However, if you do something for me I can give you extra credit."

"Yeah, I'll do anything. What are we talking, like another paper or something?"

"No, I'm not reading another one of your papers. As you know the final is a 50 question test and a three page paper. You will give me a blank scantron with your name on it, I will fill in the answers and give you an A on the test. Then I will go easy on you when I read your paper. Don't worry. I will make sure Hanover won't even notice."

"So you will help me cheat?" I ask, thinking this is some kind of trick.

"Yes."

I sit there quietly as I try to process what had just been said. "What do you want in return?"

"Hmm," she says touching her finger to her chin and looking up to the ceiling. "How much do you think a passing grade in a class you desperately need to pass is worth?" She sees that I don't know how to answer and gives me a mischievous smile. "Well I guess you don't know so I'm just going to throw out a number. $1,000."

I wait a second to answer. "Yeah, I can do that."

"Good, because it's going to be $2,000."

"Two thousand! But you just said $1,000."

"Yeah, that's before you were willing to pay a thousand."

"Well yeah but," I start before she cuts me off.

Raising her hands up, "Listen, take it or leave it. Good luck passing without my help." She stands up.

"I'll take it!" I say quickly. I fall back in my chair.

"Good. Bring me the money next week." She gives my hand a tap. "Oh, and just in case you are wondering, you say anything I will fail you. And don't think you can get Hanover to believe that this happened," she says rubbing her hand on her side. "You don't have a chance." She gives me a wink and a smile. "See you next week Tyler."

"Bye."

Another $2,000 on this stupid class, but at least I know that I'm going to pass. The next week I give her the money and the blank scantron with my name on it so she could fill it in. Even though I had paid for an A, I am still worried that she might renege on our deal. I study for two weeks for that final, going over every note and every word in that textbook a dozen times.

When the day to take the final does come, I go through it like crazy. Every question is super easy and I breeze through all the questions, very confident that I did well on it. As I finish it, I think about the $2,000 I paid to ace this final. I think that I aced the scantron part. Did I just waste $2,000 on a grade I was already going to get? I start writing the essay part of the final. It's there that my hand starts to shake. I struggle to answer the question. Is it nerves or do I truly not understand what to write? It takes me just 30 minutes to do the scantron but the other hour and half is spent struggling on this three-page essay.

The teacher calls time and has the last remaining students turn in the test. My hands shake as I walk to the front and drop off my paper. I thank the teacher, even though I'm not thankful, and leave.

The next week is one of the most nerve-wracking weeks of my life. I have to double my prescription regimen because my herpes was acting up thanks to all the stress. I get online to see my final grade. 83%. Final grade. I let out a sigh of relief.

I am a college graduate.

Chapter 19

Five years being tortured with mindless assignments and knowledge that I will never use has finally come to an end. Too long I have been paying a grotesque sum of money for an education that I was forced to endure, because of my parents.

Here I sit at the Student Center front desk, a job that I have worked for three years now. In that time I wager I have watched nearly twenty complete series of television shows and over thirty movies. I have taken over two hundred extended lunches and shown up late for work nearly the same number of times. I am paid minimum wage for my services and loathe nearly every second of my time here. If it weren't for online streaming I would have never survived this menial task.

I look at the plain grey-blue walls. This is the second to last day that I'm scheduled to work, and then it's graduation and then life. I am moving out of my apartment next Monday, then up north to spend a week or two with my uncle until I can find a job. Now that I got that piece of paper I should easily get a job that requires a tie. That first week or two will be tough. My uncle doesn't have a spare room so I will be sleeping on his couch. It shouldn't be that difficult to find a job in a big city like Los Angeles. I have already done some job hunting and saw a lot of entry-level positions available. When I move up there I will start applying and start my life, away from both school and my parents.

"Dude! Tyler," says Joel, interrupting my daydreaming. "How excited are you? Graduation in two days! You got to be pumped."

"Yeah," I say, wishing to get back to doing nothing.

"So what do you think about coming back here?" he asks.

"What?" I glare at him.

"Now that you got your degree I can get you a job as my assistant. Job pays $13 an hour, with pretty decent benefits. Plus after a year or two, when I get promoted you can take over my job."

"I don't think so Joel."

"Come on Tyler. It would be awesome to continue working with each other." He slaps the back of my chair hard pushing me forward, and then shakes my shoulder with his hands.

It was like he stabbed me with a knife. I jump from my seat and push his hands off me. "Don't touch me!" I screamed.

"Whoa, Tyler, I was just messing with you," Joel says, concerned, as if he thought he hurt me.

"You know what? Forget it. I'm out." I push pass him and make my way to the door.

"Tyler what's wrong?" he asks, following me.

"For the last three years you have driven me crazy. Your annoying singing, your constant need to hang out, and you always have to touch my shoulders when you see me. I put up with it because this was an easy job. Pretending to be your friend got me long lunches and I could do anything and you wouldn't dare fire your friend." My words take their toll on Joel as his concern for me turn to sadness. "I'm done with school and this place." I turn and reached for the door handle.

"Hey, you can't leave yet," he said as if he didn't understand what I was saying. "You have two more hours left on the clock."

I drop my head in utter disbelief at his inability to understand the situation. "I don't care."

"O-okay, see you tomorrow."

I open the door and stand just outside the doorframe with my foot holding the door open. "I quit moron." With that I gave him the double bird and back out of the building.

The next three days become a blur of drinking and parties. No school, no work, and no responsibilities. Just fun. I miss graduation, but I don't really care. My grandparents couldn't make it out and I still haven't talked to my parents since they told me that they wouldn't pay for half my tuition like they promised. My uncle said he would come down but I told him I didn't want to walk in the ceremony.

I pack up my stuff and throw my mattress by the dumpsters. I go back in to say goodbye to Sid but he wasn't there. He had been a dick lately so I am actually happy he isn't there. Looking around the apartment to see if I missed anything, two things pop into my mind as I pass Sid's room. The girl that use to sleep there, and the security deposit. Apartment complexes always screw you out of them, so why not have a little fun. I went into Sid's room and pulled back his bed a few feet. Looking at the bottom of the wall I leaned forward and kicked my foot into the wall. Three kicks is how many it took to get my foot though. I move the bed back and leave.

I get to my uncle's place in Agoura Hills, north of LA, and he takes me out to a bar and we get trashed. A cab has to take us back to the house. I spend my first night on the most uncomfortable couch in the world, but I didn't know that until I woke up that morning. My back is killing me. I walk into the kitchen, where my uncle is at the table watching a small TV. I yawn and he turns quickly as if he had forgotten I was there.

"Hey, kid," says my Uncle, finishing what was left of his coffee. "How'd you sleep?"

"Not bad," I say, not wanting to complain.

"Cool." He looks at the clock on the oven, gets up from his chair and put his cup in the sink. "I got to get to work. So, good luck finding a job."

"Later."

That day I apply online for three jobs in the same clothes I wore last night. When I finish I jump in the shower and wait for one of the companies to call. They don't. For the next three weeks I apply and apply. With each passing day my desperation for a job grows. At first I look for jobs that pay at least $25 an hour, then $20, then $15.

I have noticed something. When companies say entry-level position, what they are really mean is entry into the company position. To receive the honor of working for their "prestigious" company you must have several years of experience and then be grateful to take a few dollars over minimum wage with no health benefits whatsoever. Seriously?

In three weeks I have applied for nearly 70 jobs and gone to one interview, and that was for a telemarketing job for $10 an hour. Fifty people showed up. People from 20 years old to 65 years old were there. Apparently after a two minute interview, they can tell who is right for the position.

I spend six weeks living with my uncle, doing the same thing ever single day. Wake up. Apply for jobs. Go to bed. At first my uncle is supportive, but now he seems to be avoiding me. I even catch him sneaking out of the house while he thought I was sleeping just so he wouldn't have to talk to me.

He gets home late tonight. I just finished making myself some pasta and was putting the dishes in the sink. He has his suit jacket in his left arm and his tie in his hand.

"Listen T," he says, leaning against the doorframe. "It's been great having you here but I don't know how much longer you can stay."

"Yeah, I'm sorry. Finding a job's been a lot more difficult but I bet I will find one soon."

"I don't know, like eight weeks here and you can't find something?" I want to tell him it's only been six but I refrain from saying anything. "Come on. Illegals get jobs at fast food places! Why can't find something like that?"

"Well, I'm not going to work fast food. I have a freaking degree. That's work for idiots."

"Those idiots have jobs." He pauses and rubs his arm. "You got a week more and you're out." He starts to turn away from me.

"What?"

"You heard me, job or not, you're out."

"Come on, I can't get an apartment with no job. I'll have nowhere to live."

"Just go home then," he says, walking out of the kitchen.

A week later I find my two suitcases next to my car. No job, no home, and a piece of paper that is just a piece paper.

Epilogue

A month ago I went on a job interview. I was there for over two hours and talked to four different people. It's amazing how in-depth an interview could go for such a simple warehouse position. I couldn't understand what happened. I was qualified and I wanted the job yet they weren't willing to give me the job. The owner was telling me that he expected me to leave after a few weeks. No matter how many times I told him that I wanted to work for the company he could not understand how someone with a degree in business would want a job as a warehouse guy. Apparently "the economy sucks" is not a good reason.

The next day I get a call from someone in Human Resources saying that they had filled the position. Apparently I am over-qualified to work.

I have lost all traces of self-worth. Not only did I have to crawl back to Utah and beg my parents to let me come home, but I'm also back working at the same department store I worked at before I went to college.

My manager is a real dick. He has me work 38 hours a week but schedules me so it's 76 hours over a ten day period. A couple hours short of full time and benefits, and just long enough to make me feel worthless.

Rickie, the stoner that came to this store right before I left for college, is the assistant manager. He has been working here for the last five years and now is number two in the entire store. He makes $72,000 a year with full benefits, and he loves to remind me of that. He schedules my breaks to coincide with his and spends the time just torturing me with his success. This guy, who's still a stoner, who has no degree, has a high paying job, and just bought his own house, while I, a college graduate, have to live with my parents and work for $9.25 an hour.

I am $251,983 in debt.

I left for college with no debt and an $8 an hour job. I left college with over $250,000 in debt for a $9.25 an hour job. For thirty years I will work just to pay off that student loan. I cannot declare bankruptcy because of student loans. It will be with me for my entire life. I am screwed.

Five Years Wasted.

www.ingramcontent.com/pod-product-compliance
Lightning Source LLC
Chambersburg PA
CBHW060432180626
46817CB00007B/2781